. . . the dangers of the island?

# replica

# Return of the Perfect Girls

## MARILYN KAYE

BANTAM BOOKS
NEW YORK · TORONTO · LONDON · SYDNEY · AUCKLAND

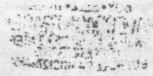

RL 5.5, 008–012

RETURN OF THE PERFECT GIRLS

A Bantam Skylark Book / June 2001

ISBN 0-553-48746-9

**Visit us on the Web! www.randomhouse.com/kids**

Published simultaneously in the United States and Canada

Bantam Skylark is an imprint of Random House Children's Books, a division of Random House, Inc. SKYLARK BOOK and colophon and BANTAM BOOKS and colophon are registered trademarks of Random House, Inc. Bantam Books, 1540 Broadway, New York, New York 10036.

PRINTED IN THE UNITED STATES OF AMERICA

OPM    10   9   8   7   6   5   4   3   2   1

For Isabelle Duquesne Clerc,
who is a really perfect girl

# Return of the Perfect Girls

# one

Amy Candler opened her bedroom window and gazed out at the early morning with satisfaction. It was going to be a perfect day.

First of all, it was a Saturday—no school and no schedule, no special chores or errands to run. The sun was shining, the sky was blue. There wasn't a cloud in sight; there wasn't even a slim chance of an unexpected shower. The air was warm but not uncomfortably hot, and there was barely a trace of humidity.

Amy took a deep breath. For a second, she thought she caught a whiff of salt water.

Of course, that was just her imagination. Even with

her highly acute sense of smell, and despite the fact that the Pacific Ocean wasn't very far away, there was no way the scent of the ocean could penetrate this far inside the metropolis of Los Angeles.

But it wouldn't be long before she'd really be breathing in that lovely salty aroma. Just an hour or so from now. With that in mind, she left the window and went to her closet for her backpack. She stuffed a towel inside and tossed in suntan lotion, a hairbrush, a bathing cap, and her camera. She was in the process of choosing between three swimsuits when she heard her mother call from downstairs.

"Amy, I'm leaving."

"Okay, Mom," she called back.

Then came the question she dreaded. "What are you up to today?" Nancy Candler wanted to know.

Amy hesitated, debated, and finally replied, "Just hanging out with Chris."

She heaved a sigh of relief when there was no further interrogation. Her mother merely responded with "Have fun," to which Amy echoed, "You too."

As she heard the car backing out of the driveway, she assured herself that she hadn't really lied to her mother. She *was* planning to spend the day with Chris Skinner, her new boyfriend. What she had neglected to mention was their destination, and the fact that they would be traveling there on a boat.

Actually, she herself didn't know the destination—that was part of the surprise.

The note had been sticking out of her locker door at school yesterday, after her last class. *Mr. Christopher Skinner cordially invites Miss Amy Candler on a mystery cruise,* it began. This was followed by a date and a time, and directions to the wharf where the boat was docked.

Amy had no idea where, how, or why Chris had managed to get his hands on a boat. He didn't usually ask her to do things by way of a formal invitation. But even though she hadn't known Chris all that long, the one thing she *did* know about him was that he was full of surprises.

She imagined that they would be going to some secluded, remote beach for a picnic, a swim, and a long, lazy day in the sun. It would be a nice change from the popular, crowded beaches where she normally went with friends. And even if Nancy Candler knew what she was up to, Amy doubted that her mother would mind. She liked Chris. He was the responsible type. Amy had no doubt that he'd make sure their adventure would be a safe one, and that she'd be back home at a reasonable hour.

She checked her watch. It was time to take off.

Almost an hour later, and after three bus changes, she was finally walking along the wharf. There were no beaches along this stretch of shore—it was more like one big, wet parking lot for boats. Crafts of all types, shapes, and sizes bobbed in the water alongside the piers that stretched out from the shore. She wasn't sure what kind of boat she was looking for, but she had a name—*Master of the Waves*. She supposed she would just have to look at every boat until she found the one with those words painted on its side.

It turned out to be a small yacht, with sleeping quarters under the deck. She'd been on one like it once before, with her mother and some friends of hers. She wondered who it belonged to, and who would be in charge of the trip. She didn't see anyone around.

Carefully, Amy stepped onto the deck. "Chris?" she called. There was no response.

He was probably waiting for her belowdecks, she decided. She located the stairs and started down. "Chris?" she called again. "Are you there?" Hearing nothing, Amy steeled herself for the possibility that he would jump out from behind something to surprise her.

Cautiously, she explored the sleeping quarters, but no one was in them. The little kitchenette was deserted too. She rapped on the door of the bathroom, but got no response.

There didn't seem to be any other place where Chris could be hiding. Apparently, she was the first to arrive.

Taking another look around, she marveled at how so much could be stuffed into such a small area. It was truly an ingenious design. A person could really live on this boat. The kitchenette had a tiny stove, a miniature refrigerator, cabinets, and a sink. A little table could be pulled down from the wall, and two stools rested under it. Every inch of space was utilized. In the bathroom, a skinny shower was neatly crammed into the corner, and the toilet was squeezed next to the sink.

She was in the process of checking out the drawers under the beds when she became aware of an odd sensation. At first, she thought the slight dizziness was the result of not eating breakfast. Then she realized that the feeling wasn't coming from inside her at all.

The boat was moving!

# two

Yes, the boat was definitely moving. Confused, Amy considered the situation. There were three possibilities: The boat could have broken loose from the pier and drifted free in the water. Or maybe Chris *was* on the boat, had seen her come aboard, and was now at the controls. Then there was the third possibility—that she had stumbled onto the wrong boat, and was about to give someone up on deck a real shock.

Keeping a hand on the railing to steady herself, Amy went back up the stairs. She could still see the shore, which was a relief—they hadn't gone too far out to sea, so maybe the person who was at the helm wouldn't be too annoyed about turning around to bring her back to the wharf.

She coughed loudly, but that didn't bring any response. "Hello?" she called out uncertainly. Surely whoever was at the helm could hear her. It had to be Chris; he was just teasing her. She had her "sea legs" now, so she made her way to the front of the boat without stumbling. She moved quietly, though—she wanted to startle Chris and get back at him for teasing her like this.

But Chris wasn't at the helm. Nor was anyone else. Amy stared at the wheel. The boat couldn't have just broken free. It wasn't bobbing on the water, it was moving, slowly but steadily—as if on some kind of automatic pilot.

"Chris, this isn't funny," Amy called out. She moved across the deck, looking behind and under anything that could be concealing him. Chris wasn't there. The boat was completely unoccupied. Except for herself, of course.

Amy extracted Chris's note from her pocket and read it again. It dawned on her that she'd never seen Chris's handwriting before. Was someone pulling a prank on her?

Uneasiness filled her, but she didn't panic. The boat wasn't going very fast, and she didn't seem to be in any immediate danger. It would be easy to dive overboard and swim to shore. An ordinary thirteen-year-old girl might find this prospect intimidating, but Amy Candler was no ordinary thirteen-year-old girl. She was one of twelve clones, genetically engineered to be physically and mentally superior to any normal human being. Swimming to shore wouldn't even tire her.

Still, Amy wondered if there were any sharks in this part of the Pacific Ocean. She knew she could swim faster than most humans, but she'd never raced a shark, and she didn't particularly want to find out who was faster.

Maybe she could figure out how to steer the boat back to shore. She went back to the helm and studied the control panel. It looked pretty complicated, and nothing was labeled. If only there was an instruction book around . . . but a search of the compartments around the wheel turned up nothing.

Then she spotted something she'd missed earlier. A piece of paper, neatly folded, was taped to the panel. She ripped it off.

*Mr. Chris Skinner awaits Miss Amy Candler in a private paradise,* she read. *Relax and enjoy the journey! P.S. There's food and drinks downstairs.*

Amy breathed a sigh of relief. At least she wouldn't be swimming with sharks today.

Chris was amazing! How had he pulled this off? She

supposed she shouldn't be too astonished by his imagination and creativity. From the moment she'd met him, she'd known he was unusual.

When he first appeared at Parkside Middle School, some kids thought he was weird. He barely spoke, he had long hair, a sullen attitude, and he always wore the same black leather jacket.

But Amy saw through his defensive mask, and found an independent, self-reliant boy who was more mature than most of the kids at school. Homeless and abandoned by his parents, Chris had been on his own for a long time. This made him different from the average middle school student, and that was enough to make some kids write him off immediately. Not Amy, though. Amy understood what it was like to feel different.

But her genetically extraordinary body couldn't ward off hunger, and the result of not eating breakfast was kicking in. She went downstairs and poked around in the little kitchen area.

In a paper bag, she discovered a fresh cinnamon bun. And in the refrigerator she found a carton of her favorite juice—cranberry apple. Chris had thought of everything!

Amy took her supplies back up to the deck and settled down on a reclining lounge chair. Gazing up at the blue sky while she sipped and ate, she felt like a princess, cruising on her yacht. It was too bad Chris wasn't here to enjoy the experience with her, but it was nice having a few minutes alone to daydream and think about what a good life she had.

She was so lucky to have found a boyfriend like Chris! Most boys his age wouldn't know how to organize a romantic outing. Her last boyfriend, Eric, never had any romantic ideas. And ever since he left middle school, he'd been acting so superior.

Then there was Andy . . . Amy wasn't sure if she could really count him as a boyfriend. He too was a genetically engineered clone, and they shared a special bond. He had even kissed her once, at the top of the Eiffel Tower in Paris. But that was a while ago, and she hadn't seen him since.

No, she definitely considered Chris Skinner her one and only boyfriend now. He was special. . . .

She yawned. Strange, it wasn't even noon and she felt like taking a nap. Maybe it was the sea air . . . and the gentle rocking of the boat.

She closed her eyes.

# three

# 3

It was one of those lovely, long, dreamless siestas, the kind of nap that you don't want to let go, even after you start to wake up. With her eyes closed, lying on the lounge chair in the warmth of the sun, swaying rhythmically on the calm sea, Amy was supremely comfortable, and she wouldn't have minded staying that way for a long time.

Only it seemed to her that she had already been in this position for a while. Reluctantly, she forced her eyes open. The sky was still blue and cloudless, but something was different . . . the sun. It wasn't directly overhead now, but more to the west. This wasn't morning anymore. How long had she been sleeping, anyway?

Languidly, she raised her arm so she could get a look at her watch. Quarter after five . . .

She sat up abruptly. Quarter after five? How could that be?

She rubbed her eyes and looked at the watch again. Unbelievable . . . she'd been sailing on this boat for almost six hours. This was crazy. What could Chris be thinking, arranging a picnic or outing or whatever this was so far from home? There was no way she'd be back before her mother that evening. Chris would have some serious explaining to do.

She wondered if something could have gone wrong with the boat. Maybe the remote mechanism, or whatever was controlling the boat, had messed up. Swinging her legs around to the side of the chair, she stood up.

She had to grab the arm of the chair to steady herself. Odd, how dizzy she was. The sensation passed quickly, but now a real uneasiness seized her. Only once before had she ever awakened feeling this unsteady—and that had been in a hospital, where she'd been given drugs. Maybe she hadn't just fallen asleep naturally. Maybe she had been *made* to sleep. Could someone have put something in the cinnamon bun, or in the cranberry apple juice? But who? Why? And where was she going?

Amy didn't have the slightest idea. But at this precise moment, she was pretty sure that this had nothing to do with a picnic and a swim and an outing at a secluded beach. In fact, she was very sure this had nothing to do with Chris.

Quickly she headed to the front of the boat and examined the wheel and the knobs and dials around it. There had to be some way she could turn this thing around and send it back to where it came from. But the mechanism looked no less complicated than it had when she'd first examined it hours earlier.

With her eyes fixed on the horizon, Amy walked around the perimeter of the boat, watching for any sign of land. Having ruled out Chris or navigational problems, her instincts told her something ominous was definitely about to unfold.

She wasn't being overly dramatic. From the moment Amy discovered what she was and how she had come to be, she'd known that trouble could follow her. Kidnapping . . . abduction . . . they weren't farfetched notions.

She saw nothing until she came full circle. Then, looking straight ahead from the steering wheel, she caught a glimpse of green. An island. The boat was heading in that direction. And it was picking up speed.

But she couldn't just stand here, waiting, allowing the boat—or whatever, whoever, guided it—to be in control of her destiny. It wasn't her nature to be passive, and she refused to be a sitting duck. She had to take charge of the situation.

She didn't waste any time. She climbed up to the top railing, took a deep breath, and dived.

The shock of ice-cold salt water wiped out any leftover effects of her siesta. She was completely alert, and she felt strong. Whatever had knocked her unconscious hadn't caused any permanent damage—just put her out of commission for a while.

But now she was back. She stroked and kicked in rhythm, and relied on her keen sense of direction to keep moving toward the island. Despite her anxiety and uncertainty, she was aware of the clear turquoise of the water, the coral reefs, the colorful fish she passed. It was beautiful. . . . Where *was* she?

When her feet touched a sandy bottom and she was able to stand up, the view gave her no greater insight as to her whereabouts. Her location remained a mystery. But if she had to make a guess, she decided she'd just arrived at one of those islands advertised on travel agency posters. This was the kind of island that would typically be named Paradise or the Garden of Eden.

The beach was pristine—white and totally empty. The sand was warm and soft, like powder. Crossing the beach, Amy found herself approaching large rocks that formed a stairway, and she climbed upward. A path made of tiny pebbles led her toward an area where leafy trees provided natural protection from the hot sun. The trees became denser, and she found herself in a woods.

She looked back toward the shore and saw the boat. She would have ended up here anyway, even if she hadn't jumped off and swum to shore. But at least she'd arrived on her own terms—mainly, wet.

Standing very still, she concentrated on listening. There was the rustling of leaves, the faint call of seagulls—and voices. Yes, the light breeze carried just the faintest hint of human voices. She couldn't make out anything specific, but she followed the sound, and as she did, she made out more voices. Music, too.

As the sounds became more distinct, Amy moved more slowly, more cautiously. She emerged from the woods to find a wall of rocks—and she knew the sounds were coming from the other side.

She examined the wall, searching for a crack or space

that she could peer through. When she found one, she pressed herself against it. She made out figures . . . ten . . . no, eleven. As she concentrated her vision, the figures came into focus. Girls . . . they were all girls. They all seemed to be about the same age, the same height . . .

And they all looked like her.

# four

A slow chill crept up Amy's spine. She looked again to make sure she wasn't mistaken. No, her vision hadn't failed her. Those were her clones out there. And that could only mean one thing.

"Number Seven."

Amy whirled around. A very tall, slender, absolutely beautiful woman stood there, dressed in a snug-fitting olive green unitard. With her long, wavy brown hair and her high cheekbones, she looked like a supermodel.

Amy's gaze swept over her. The woman did not appear to be armed. Her full lips were curled into a wide smile. She looked harmless, even kind, not threatening at all.

But Amy knew that appearances could be deceiving. And having seen what—who—waited behind the stone wall, she knew who this woman was—or at least, where she came from. As the realization hit her, Amy knew fear of a kind that she hadn't felt for a long time. But pride, if nothing else, forbade her from letting this woman see just how stunned and frightened she really was. Somehow, she managed to keep her expression stoic and her voice steady.

"I know who you are," she said.

The woman continued to smile, but her arched eyebrows rose. "You do? We've never met. My name is Cindy."

"You're with the organization," Amy accused her. "You've finally found us, all of us, all the Amys, and you've brought us to this island. We're trapped here, aren't we?"

She expected "Cindy" to fake innocence and deny any knowledge of what Amy was talking about. But the beautiful woman just nodded.

"That's right, Number Seven. Now, come and meet your sisters."

Amy's eyes darted around. How many other organization people were there? Could she take them all on? What was the best escape route?

"You can't get away, Number Seven," Cindy said. "And before you try, why not hear what I have to say? Maybe then you won't want to leave."

Amy doubted that—but she didn't have any options at the moment. And although she was undeniably scared, she couldn't help feeling curious, too. She followed the woman around the stone wall to an opening. As they entered the enclosure, the other clones turned toward them. Amy searched their faces, looking for signs of recognition.

Expressions varied. There was fear on some faces, anger on others. There were cautious Amys, watchful Amys, hostile Amys. . . .

Amy had met some of them before, and she tried to identify them now. It wasn't easy. Hairstyles and hair colors could have changed since their last encounter, and their clothing didn't provide any clues. But including her, there were twelve, so all of the ones she knew had to be among them. Like Aimee, the actress. Annie, the French ballet dancer. There were the Amys she remembered from the nightmare of New York, the ones who had been with her in the hospital. Like Amy, Number Eight, who talked tough but was sweet inside, and Amy, Number Five, the collaborator, who had been working with the organization against her own sisters . . . but at this point, it was impossible to know who was who.

Then Amy remembered something else about the New York experience. Someone had died there. Number Three, the timid girl from the farm . . . Amy herself had seen the body lying under a blanket on a table. So how could there be twelve Amys here?

*Aly.* Number Thirteen. The defective clone, the discarded clone, the reject clone who had been put up for adoption while the others were still being nurtured in their incubators. Aly Kendricks had to be among these girls.

Memories flooded back. Seeing Aly for the first time at the carnival, meeting her at the skating rink. On the phone, exchanging e-mails. Staying overnight at each other's homes, giggling and acting silly and being like sisters.

Funny, cheerful, completely normal Aly, who believed that she and Amy were twins who had been separated at birth. Aly wanted so very much to be like Amy and couldn't understand why she never would be. When her desperate attempts to imitate her clone threatened her own life, Aly's parents and Amy's mother saw the danger in the relationship. The Kendricks family moved away, and Amy hadn't seen her normal replica since.

Which one was she? The one who looked totally out of it, completely bewildered? The one who seemed almost excited? The one with the red eyes, who looked as if she'd been crying?

Amy flinched as Cindy placed a hand lightly on her shoulder. "Here she is, last but not least, Number Seven," the woman announced to the group.

"Now we can begin."

# f5ve

As the girls drew closer, Cindy enveloped them in a wide, warm smile. This broke the uneasy silence and released a cacophony of voices.

"What's going on?"

"What are we doing here?"

And a particularly shrill voice cried out, "This is supposed to be a shoot for a television commercial! Where are the cameras? Where's my hairdresser? I demand to see my agent!"

Cindy raised her hands in a calming gesture. "All your questions will be answered," she assured the group. "But first of all, I want you all to know, you have absolutely nothing to worry about. The organization is going to take very good care of you."

Her words did nothing to reassure Amy—in fact, they sent icicles sliding down her back. She turned to look at the other girls around her. Were they reacting in the same way? Did they know what she did about the organization?

Clearly, at least one of them seemed to. The girl standing closest to Amy uttered a short laugh. "I am *so* not believing that."

Cindy's smile didn't flicker. "Why?"

"Because I remember what you did to us in the hospital in New York," the clone shot back.

"I remember the hospital too," Amy called out. There were murmurs of agreement from other girls.

The corners of Cindy's smile shifted downward, and she gave a sad frown. "That was a mistake," she told them. "Those people have all been dismissed. There have been many changes within the organization. Just as you all have experienced many changes recently. Look at you! You're not children anymore. You've come of age, you are young women. And by now, you know that you are not like other people."

Someone's expression must have indicated confusion, because Cindy seemed surprised. "Surely, with your intelligence, by now you've figured it out. No?" She sighed.

"All right, I'm going to run through it once. Maybe it's better this way. I can clear up any misconceptions you have."

She gestured for the girls to take seats on the smooth rocks. Amy sat down, watching Cindy carefully and wondering what kind of fairy tale they were about to hear.

*She* knew the whole story, of course, probably better than the others. After all, her own mother had been one of the scientists involved in the cloning procedure. But she sat cross-legged, said nothing, and waited to hear the organization's version of Project Crescent.

"Thirteen years ago," Cindy began, "a group of visionaries had a dream. They believed that new genetic technologies could be employed to improve the human race. By combining genetic material and altering the DNA, they created a prototype that they were able to duplicate. Their goal was to bring humanity to a level of physical, intellectual, and emotional perfection."

Cindy was making it sound like a holy mission, and Amy couldn't bear the thought that some of the clones might be buying this explanation. She offered some additional information about the organization's goals. "And take over the world."

Cindy gazed at her reprovingly. "Unfortunately, that's what some of the scientists believed. They took it upon themselves to destroy the project, and they tried to convince the organization that the genetically altered duplicates had been eliminated in the process. Our organization had doubts, and continued to investigate. We kept track of the scientists, so that we could—"

Amy broke in again. "So that you could kill them. And you succeeded in killing the director, Dr. Jaleski."

Cindy was becoming annoyed. "Number Seven, please stop interrupting. As I was saying, we traced the scientists, and eventually we were able to discover what they did with the clones. You were distributed throughout the world, and put up for adoption. For years, we have searched for you. Today . . . today, we have finally succeeded in bringing you all back together."

"Why?" Amy demanded. "What do you want from us?"

A voice very similar to her own spoke from behind her. "Why don't you shut up for a minute and maybe she'll tell us?"

"We've brought you here to help you realize your potential," Cindy declared. "You will learn how very special you are. We will teach you how to exploit your amazing talents and abilities to make this world a better place for all people."

An Amy leaped to her feet. "What gives you the

right to do this? You've brought us here against our will! Do our parents know what you've done?"

"Don't be silly, Number Eight," Cindy chastised her. "First of all, your parents aren't even your real parents, they're just the people who have taken care of you. You are above and beyond them now. You don't need them anymore."

There were gasps, and cries of dismay. "You mean we'll never see our families again?" someone asked, and there was the unmistakable sound of a muffled sob.

Cindy was exasperated. "Our observations have convinced us that you are all in excellent physical shape and that your intellectual skills are far beyond normal. But I can see that you still have a long way to go before you achieve emotional perfection."

"Are we supposed to be happy about this?" one clone shrieked.

Cindy had clearly had it. "Yes!" she yelled back. "Good grief, look around you! You're on a beautiful island where all your needs will be taken care of. Most of you have probably spent your lives hiding your gifts, afraid of letting anyone see how athletic or smart you are. Here, you are with your sisters! You're free to be who you are! You can relax and enjoy yourselves!"

Amy couldn't believe what this woman was trying to

pull on them. "You're making it sound like you're doing us a favor, like you've brought us on a vacation! This is kidnapping!"

"Nonsense," Cindy said. "How could we kidnap what already belongs to us?"

The impact of this statement hit them all simultaneously, and the words were greeted by a horrified silence. Cindy appeared to be satisfied with the reaction.

"I think that's all you need to know for today," she said. "You've had a long trip; you must be tired and hungry. We'll be serving dinner now, and then you'll be taken to your lovely cabins for the evening. Tomorrow morning, we'll begin our real work. But don't worry. It's going to be fun!"

She beckoned for the girls to follow her down a path that led out of the natural amphitheater. As Amy rose, she spoke to the girl who had come alongside her.

"Cindy sounds like all those teachers who tell you learning can be fun," she muttered. "I never trusted any of them either."

The clone smiled. "Oh, I think we can trust her. She seems to have a true understanding of our natural superiority. Perhaps now you too will learn to appreciate this."

This Amy spoke in a charming French accent. She tossed her hair and hurried ahead on the light feet of a ballerina. So now Amy knew she had identified Annie Perrault, who believed that the world should rid itself of people who didn't meet her standards. Amy recalled the unpleasant encounters they'd had in the Catacombs of Paris.

As for the others, the one who'd demanded to speak to her agent had to be Aimee, the spoiled and self-centered actress. Amy had met her when the girl filmed a horror movie on the grounds of Parkside Middle School. The loudmouth was definitely Number Eight, from New York. The one who had ordered Amy to shut up—that could have been Number Five, Amy's chief competition for leadership back at the hospital.

And somewhere among the others was Aly, Number Thirteen. Who didn't belong there at all.

**six**

I t wasn't exactly a luxury hotel room, but it wasn't bad. Sitting on the single bed, Amy took stock of her surroundings.

The girls had been taken to a row of twelve identical cabins. Each was given a cabin of her own, and Amy assumed that each cabin was the same. There were a bed, a small table and chair, and a chest of drawers. Inside the chest, she'd found clothes, all new—underwear, jeans, shorts, T-shirts, pajamas.

A pair of heavy-duty athletic shoes stood on the floor beside the chest. Everything was in the correct size. That didn't surprise her. If the organization actually *had* been monitoring them for years, they would know precisely how big the clones were now.

In the small attached bathroom, Amy found a toothbrush, toothpaste, soap, shampoo—all the standard toiletries. The organization appeared to have thought of everything the girls might need.

Suddenly Amy wondered if she was being watched. There could be video cameras hidden in the room, recording every move she made, any attempt to escape. She also wondered if she was the only one who wasn't sleeping.

She listened intently for any noise that would indicate another clone who was awake. She was rewarded with the faint sound of a sob. Someone was crying.

Amy hopped off her bed and went to the door. Testing the doorknob, she saw that they weren't in a jail—the door wasn't locked, and when she opened it a crack, she didn't see any guards posted outside. It would be easy to walk out and keep going.

But where to? She didn't think she'd get very far. The organization wouldn't have gone to all this trouble of setting up a private island paradise for the clones just to let them stroll away. Besides, they were in the middle of an ocean, and even a physically superior being couldn't swim hours and hours through possibly shark-infested waters.

Tentatively, Amy stepped outside, half expecting to hear alarms go off. But all was quiet. Off in the distance, waves crashed on the shore, and the warm breeze made the leaves on the trees rustle. But the only other sound she heard was the quiet weeping.

"Aly?" she whispered. "Is that you?" But then she realized that if the crying girl *was* Aly, she wouldn't hear Amy calling her. Aly didn't share the sensitive hearing of the other clones.

Amy walked along the row of cabins. Each door bore a number—her own had been #7—which she assumed matched the number of the Amy who was staying there. The Amy who had died in the hospital was Number Three, so she paused in front of cabin #3 and listened at the door.

Her hunch was right. Someone inside cabin #3 was crying.

Amy rapped softly at the door. Immediately, the crying stopped, and a small, quavering voice asked, "Who is it? What do you want?"

"Aly? Is that you?"

A second later the door was flung open. "Amy? Amy Candler?" The girl threw her arms around Amy. "I knew one of them had to be you!" she sobbed. "Oh, Amy, I knew you'd come looking for me!"

"Shhh!" Amy hissed, pushing Aly back into the cabin and shutting the door behind them.

Aly released her. "Amy, what's going on? What are we doing here? Who are all those girls who look like us?"

"Didn't you hear Cindy's explanation?" Amy asked her.

"You mean, it's true? We're clones?"

Amy nodded. "Only, Cindy had one fact wrong. There were thirteen clones, not twelve. One of the clones . . . well, she didn't work out."

"Me," Aly said.

Amy nodded. "Something went wrong. Your DNA structure didn't develop like the rest of ours."

Aly sank down on her bed. "That's why I was never able to do what you could do. I wasn't as strong, I couldn't run as fast. . . . I was a reject. I was the runt of the litter."

Amy nodded again. "Your father was the custodian in the building where Project Crescent was going on. When Dr. Jaleski, the head of the project, realized your progress wasn't the same as the other clones, he asked him to bring you to an adoption agency. But instead your dad brought you home."

Aly was silent for a minute. "Then what am I doing

here with the rest of you? If I'm not one of the elite clones, why do they want me?"

Amy told her about Number Three. "They were testing a bunch of us in a hospital in New York. Number Three died, accidentally, I think. I guess there was some sort of power struggle within the organization, and the people at the hospital aren't in charge anymore. This new group doesn't seem to know everything that happened there."

"So they think I'm Number Three," Aly said. "They think I'm like the rest of you."

"That's what it looks like," Amy admitted.

Aly began to tremble. "What—what's going to happen when they find out I'm not like you? What will they do to me?"

"I don't know," Amy said. "Because I don't know what they want with the rest of us." But she had a troubling suspicion that the organization wouldn't have any use for Aly. In which case . . . would they let her go? Or would they be concerned that she already knew too much?

"Cindy said they wouldn't hurt us," Aly murmured hopefully. "And she seems nice, don't you think?"

Amy couldn't honestly agree, but nodded anyway. Even if Cindy was telling the truth, Amy didn't know if the guarantee of safety would apply to a defective clone. Besides, she knew from experience that they couldn't trust anything these people told them.

She didn't want to tell that to Aly, though. The poor girl was already so frightened.

Aly gazed at her plaintively. "Amy . . ."

"Hmm?"

"You won't let them hurt me, will you?"

Amy gazed warmly at the girl. She hoped she sounded convincing when she said, "No, I won't let them hurt you."

"What are you going to do?"

"*We,*" Amy corrected her. "We have to work together, Aly. I want to get away from here just as much as you do."

"I'll bet all the clones feel that way," Aly said.

Amy wondered about that. She remembered how willing Number Five had been to go along with the organization back at the hospital in New York. She'd been ready to betray her sister clones. And Annie Perrault . . . Amy had a very clear memory of how proud Annie was, how she liked being superior to other people.

But they were only two of twelve. "First of all," she told Aly, "we're going to find out exactly what we're up against. I want to know how many organization people are on this island." She stood up. "Come on, let's go for a walk."

"Now? In the dark?"

"Aly, we're all going to have to be brave," Amy warned her.

"Easy for someone with super-powers to say," Aly muttered. But she got off the bed and put on her shoes.

Outside, she turned to Amy. "Which way should we go?"

Amy listened. "Do you hear that?"

"What?"

"Never mind." But Amy was definitely hearing something that wasn't natural. It was an electronic beeping. "Follow me." She moved down toward the higher cabin numbers and discovered the source of the sound alongside cabin #10.

A clone was punching buttons on a mobile phone. "Hello? Hello?" the girl was saying. Apparently, she wasn't getting any response. She began hitting more digits.

"Isn't it working?" Amy asked her.

"I don't understand," the girl said in annoyance. "This just happens to be the most expensive mobile phone in the universe. It's supposed to work everywhere."

Amy looked at the display. "Your battery is dead. When was the last time you recharged it?"

The girl looked at her in disdain. "I have people who do things like that for me."

Now Amy knew which clone this was. "You're Aimee Evans, aren't you?"

The girl affected a pose. "You recognize me!"

Amy rolled her eyes. "We all look alike, remember? Anyway, we met before. You were in a movie that was being filmed at my middle school."

Aimee's eyes narrowed. "Oh yeah, I remember you. I got fired because of you!"

"Well, don't dwell on the past," Amy said. "We're all in the same boat now." She indicated her companion. "This is Aly, Number Three. We're going to have a look around. Want to come?"

"I want to find the person in charge," Aimee declared. "This is outrageous. I'm up for a part in a series, and I have to be in Los Angeles tomorrow. If this organization or whatever it is screws up my audition, my agent is going to kill them. I want to tell them that."

Somehow, Amy doubted that the organization would tremble in fear of Aimee's agent. She didn't say this, though. She was glad to have another able-bodied clone scoping the island with them—even if it was a snotty actress.

There wasn't much light to guide them, only a sliver

of moon. The sight of the thin crescent made Amy think of something.

"You don't have a birthmark on your right shoulder, do you?" she asked Aly.

"No, why?"

"Back at the Project Crescent laboratory, the rest of us were marked with a crescent tattoo," Amy explained. She turned to Aimee. "You have one, don't you?"

"I used to," Aimee said. "I had it surgically removed."

Amy was taken aback. "Why?"

Aimee looked at her as if she was stupid. "I got bored with it."

Personally, Amy wasn't bored with her mark. And she never would be—it was a part of who she was. She wore a little charm in the same shape on a chain around her neck. Dear Dr. Jaleski had given it to her before he died. But in a way, she was pleased to hear what Aimee had done. Aly could use the same excuse if anyone wanted to know why *she* didn't have the mark.

The path they were walking was leading them into the forest. "Are you sure you know where we're going?" Aimee asked.

"No, I don't have the slightest idea where we're going," Amy told her. "That's why we all need to keep quiet and listen for sounds."

"I don't hear anything," Aly said.

"What about you?" Amy asked Aimee. As a successful genetically altered clone, Aimee would have hearing as sharp as Amy's.

"Nope."

"Concentrate harder," Amy urged.

"I'm too tired to concentrate," Aimee complained.

Amy stifled a groan. Clearly, neither of her companions was going to be much help. So she closed her eyes and tried to hear as far as she could.

There were noises, of course. Leaves rustling . . . a faint whistle . . . bird calls. At one point she heard something slithering on the ground and hoped it wasn't some sort of poisonous snake. There was also the sound of the wind. . . .

And the wind carried something else. Voices. Very, very soft, and still far off, totally indistinct . . . but definitely voices. "This way," Amy whispered to the other two, and started up an incline.

Aimee eventually stopped and sniffed. Her nose wrinkled. "What's that?"

"What's what?" Aly asked.

But Amy could smell it too. Burning wood . . . "A campfire," she said. She quickened her pace. The voices were coming from the same direction, and they were becoming more distinct. She couldn't make out what was being said, but she was able to identify something about the voices. They were male.

"How much farther?" Aimee whined.

"Shut up," Amy whispered.

Aimee was offended. "Don't tell me to shut up! Besides, whoever they are, they're too far away. They can't hear me."

Amy wasn't so sure about that. A possibility had just occurred to her—an interesting possibility that wouldn't be exactly unwelcome. But maybe it was too much to hope for. . . .

There was only one voice now, a man's voice. It was close enough for Amy to pick up some words.

". . . enough to eat . . . tired . . . your cabins . . ."

The voice faded. There was the sound of bodies standing up, walking away. The meeting was going on just over this ridge. Amy hugged a tree and peered through the foliage. What she saw made her heart leap.

Turning, she put a finger to her lips and motioned the others to come look through the leaves.

Aly gasped. "Boys!"

Aimee could see something Aly couldn't. "They all look alike!"

Amy nodded. She knew something neither of them knew.

The boys were all named Andy.

# seven

"Tell me more about those boys," Aly demanded the next morning as they walked back to the clearing. "I couldn't see their faces. How old are they? Are they cute?"

"I don't know that much about them," Amy admitted. "I've only met one of them. They were created four years before us, so they're around sixteen. And if they're all exactly alike, the way we are . . ." She thought about the Andy that she knew. "Well, they're definitely cute."

"Do they have super-powers like you and the other Amys? Are they stronger than regular people like me?"

Amy was getting uncomfortable with the direction of the conversation. "Aly, listen up. You need to keep quiet, okay? Don't ask too many questions, don't let people know you're not like the rest of us. Don't draw attention to yourself. And *don't* say anything about seeing the boys last night."

"Why not?"

"Because we want to stay one step ahead of the organization. We don't want *them* to know what *we* know."

Aly was puzzled. "You mean, you think they don't know those boys are here on the island?"

She'd forgotten that Aly didn't have the superior IQ of the other clones—in fact, she wasn't even quite sure that Aly was up to the *average* level of human intelligence. "I'm sure they know about the Andys," Amy told her. "But they don't have to know that *we* know about them. Get it?"

"I think so," Aly said uncertainly.

They reached the meeting place, and Amy immediately realized that the presence of the boys couldn't be kept a secret. Apparently, word had already spread, and the group was buzzing.

"*Boys!*" one of the girls was squealing. "A whole bunch of them! And I heard they're really hot!"

"Are they here for us?" another one was wondering

out loud. "Like, to hang with? That could be so very cool!"

"Are you guys totally whacked?" a clone standing near Amy blurted. "Just because there are boys here, you're happy now? You think this is some kind of holiday?"

"There are blueberry muffins for breakfast, too," another Amy pointed out, as if that was the frosting on the vacation cake.

"I can't believe you guys," the girl exclaimed. "You're willing to be held prisoners as long as you've got stud puppies and blueberry muffins? You're *sick!*"

Amy turned to her. "You're Number Eight, right?"

The girl nodded. "Amy Sherman, Brooklyn, New York. Who are you?"

"Amy Candler. Number Seven, from Los Angeles."

Eight's eyebrows went up. "You were at the hospital."

"Right." And we were on the same side there, Amy wanted to add, but she didn't think it was a good time to say that. Number Five could be listening to them.

It was a pain, not being able to tell them apart. And now that they were all wearing identical jeans and T-shirts, it would be next to impossible. Aimee, the actress, had her hair colored lighter than the others, a couple of girls wore their hair short, and one had bangs, but that was about it as far as distinctions between them. The same height, the same weight, the same features—Amy wondered if she'd ever get used to seeing herself all over the place.

The clones were settling down with their muffins and juice while Cindy mingled among them. Two girls were helping Cindy distribute the food—bland-looking identical twins who looked familiar. Number Eight recognized them first.

"They were at the hospital, too," she reminded Amy. "The zombies in the pink smocks, remember?"

Amy remembered. These girls were the result of an early cloning effort, with bodies that worked perfectly but minds that were incapable of complex thought or decision making.

So some elements of the organization hadn't changed, she thought. Of course, the pink-smock girls wouldn't have anything to do with the power struggle that had taken place. At the hospital, they'd been like robots, following orders and showing no intellectual or emotional responses to anything going on around them.

Amy wondered if the other Amys who had been at the hospital had noticed their presence here. It didn't look like it. They were too busy speculating about the rumor of boys on the island. By now, Cindy had picked up on the gossip.

"How did you find out about the boys?" she asked one of the girls.

Amy waited apprehensively. She didn't particularly want Cindy to know she and two others had been snooping around. Fortunately, the Amy who'd been questioned wasn't specific. "Someone saw them, I guess. Who are they? Are they clones?"

Apparently, Cindy didn't think there was any point in keeping the Andys a secret. "Yes, they're just like you. Well, not exactly like you. Because they're boys, of course!" She giggled a little, as if she thought the Amys might not be aware of the difference between boys and girls. Then she added, "And since they were created four years before you, they're physically more mature. But since genetic advancements were made in the period between the two projects, you girls have certain superior qualities."

Well, that was interesting. Amy wondered if Andy knew about these differences. And she wondered what these superior qualities were. Were the girls smarter than the boys? Did they have keener hearing or eyesight?

Cindy didn't explain. "Don't rely on your natural superiority in the upcoming competitions, however! That's right, we're going to be holding competitions between you and the boys. It should be challenging and revealing at the same time. I think you'll find that, all things considered, you'll be equally matched."

She explained that the island competitions would involve two teams—the Amy group versus the Andy group—and that the events would range from physical to intellectual to creative and emotional challenges.

"Are there prizes for the team that wins?" someone asked.

"Absolutely," Cindy assured her. "There will be all kinds of special treats for the winning team."

"And the team that loses?" another Amy wanted to know. "What happens to them?"

"The team that loses a challenge will lose a teammate," Cindy informed them.

Amy didn't like the sound of that. "What do you mean, 'lose a teammate'?" she asked.

Cindy explained. "After each competition, the losing team will meet back at their gathering place. A secret vote will be taken among you, and the team will decide who is to be let go. Naturally, you'll want to lose your least significant member and hold on to your more valuable ones. So this should provide each of you with the motivation to do your very best!"

"It sounds like that TV show," Number Eight whispered to Amy.

Amy knew what she was talking about—*Survivor*.

Clearly, all the girls had watched the show or at least heard of it, because there was another excited buzz of conversation.

"Does the last person left get a million dollars?" someone wanted to know.

Cindy just smiled. "The last person remaining will have a very handsome reward."

"I do not know of this television show." That statement was declared in a French accent.

Someone asked Annie Perrault, "Didn't you have *Survivor* in France?"

"No. What happened to the people who were voted to go away?"

"They went home," Aly told her. She turned to Cindy. "Is that what happens to us when we get voted off the island? We go home?"

Cindy looked at her reprovingly. "Right now, you should be thinking about how to stay *on* the island, not what happens if you leave."

Aly whispered in Amy's ear. "I'll bet I'm the first one voted off. You know I won't be as good as you guys."

Amy knew Aly was probably right. Which was why she too wanted to know what happened to the team members who were voted off the island. But obviously Cindy wasn't prepared to answer that question right now, and Amy didn't want to bug her. If Amy was going to help Aly get through this experience, she'd be spending a lot of time by her side—so she didn't need to draw Cindy's attention to herself any more than Aly did.

The other girls were wolfing down their muffins and commenting on how good they were. Amy took a tiny bite of hers. It *was* good—but that didn't make her feel any better. For all she knew, everything they were eating could be poisoned or treated with drugs. But what were her options—starving herself?

It was a relief to learn that their first challenge had to do with gathering natural food.

"This is a test to see how well you can take care of yourselves in a wild environment," Cindy told them. "You will be given a certain amount of time to search the woods and beaches for food. The boys are being given the same assignment. The team that brings in the largest quantity of edible items is the winner."

"What's the prize?" an Amy asked.

"The prize is the food you gather," Cindy told them. "What you find will be your lunch. And you won't get anything else to eat until dinnertime. That should be enough to motivate you!" She looked at her watch. "You can begin your expedition in ten minutes. Be back here at noon." She started to leave the enclosure.

"Wait a minute!" Aimee called. "You mean, we have to find our own food? How do we do that?"

"You'll have to figure it out yourselves," Cindy said. "That's one of the goals of this island experience. You will learn to work together as a team. I'm sure that if you all put your heads together, you'll come up with a plan." She strode out of the enclosure without looking back, leaving behind twelve puzzled clones.

"Are we supposed to eat dirty weeds and stuff?" one girl wailed. "Do we have to kill animals?"

"I'll bet there's poison ivy out there," another Amy said, shuddering as she gazed out at the wooded area. "And poison mushrooms, and poison berries. Does anyone know how to tell if something's poisonous?"

Amy felt a tug on her sleeve. "I've been in Girl Scouts," Aly whispered. "I know all about that stuff."

The other girls' acute hearing caused them all to look at Aly.

"Which one are you?" The question came from the clone with the fringe of straight hair that hung over her eyebrows.

"I'm Number . . ." Aly hesitated and turned to Amy helplessly, having forgotten who she was replacing. Amy quickly provided the answer before anyone could notice Aly's uncertainty.

"Three! Hey guys, this is great. Three can show us which berries and nuts are okay to eat." She beamed proudly at Aly.

"Then you're the leader of this mission," the Amy-with-bangs declared. "You're in charge."

That was when Amy recognized the confident, assured tone of that particular "sister." She had to be Number Five. Even though she wasn't taking charge herself, she was making the decisions.

The other Amys seemed perfectly willing to accept that. They were all watching Aly and waiting for her to start giving directions. Aly looked completely confused.

Amy jumped in again. "I'll bet I can guess what you're going to say," she said quickly. "Cindy said that the team with the most food wins, right? If we all stay together, we won't be able to cover that much area. So we should divide up into groups of three or four. And you should tell us what not to pick. Once we've gathered as much food as possible, by no later than eleven-thirty, we should meet back here. Then you'll look at all the stuff and take out what's not edible. Right, Aly?"

"Right," Aly echoed faintly.

Everyone watched her expectantly. Fortunately, having been in a Girl Scout troop and involved in Scouting activities, Aly remembered something about organizing teams.

"We should count off," she said. "To put ourselves in

groups. One, two, three, four, like that, so each group will have four people."

"You mean three people," someone said. "Four into twelve is three."

"Oh yeah," Aly said. "Right. I've always had trouble with multiplication. I mean, division."

"One!" Amy called out quickly, and Number Eight immediately followed with "Two!"

The others continued counting off, until they had four groups of three each. At Amy's urging, Aly then described what poisonous mushrooms looked like. Amy was pleased with the way the others were paying attention to Aly. She had no doubt that on this mission, Aly would prove herself valuable to the team. The other girls were watching her and listening to her with evident respect.

Except for one—the one with the bangs. She was looking at Amy. And Amy could see something in her expression that she wouldn't call respect. It was more like . . . suspicion.

# e8ght

"What about these berries?" Number Eleven bent down to examine a patch of red fruit at the base of a tree. "Look, Number Seven."

Amy looked down in the same direction. "I thought Aly, I mean, Number Three said no red berries are safe."

"Only if they're perfectly round," Number Eleven reminded her. "These are wide at the top and more narrow at the bottom. I think they might be wild strawberries. She said those would be okay to eat." She turned to Aimee. "Isn't that what Three said, Number—what *is* your number, anyway?"

"I'm not a number," was the chilly reply. "I'm Aimee Evans, for crying out loud. I'm *famous*."

Eleven responded in a voice that was just as cold. "You're not *that* famous. I can only remember seeing you in one crummy commercial, and that was *ages* ago."

"For your information, I've been in *four* commercials," Aimee shot back. "Plus two miniseries. And my movie comes out next month."

"Well, la-de-da for you, Number Whatever," Eleven muttered. "Right now, all I want to know about is whether or not these are wild strawberries and if we can eat them."

Amy knelt down to take a closer look. "I think they're worth picking, and we'll let Three take a look at them. Aimee, whatever number you are, can you see any more like these around?"

"No."

Aggravated, Amy glared at her. "You're not even trying. Are you really using your ability to see? You have to concentrate."

"It gives me a headache," Aimee said.

"We don't get headaches," Eleven informed her. "None of the Amys do, we're too healthy. And you're no different from anyone else here. Even if you think you're hot stuff. And you'd better figure out what number you are, because there's no way I'm calling you by the same name that we all have."

"We don't *all* have the same name," Aimee said. "That French girl, *her* name isn't Amy."

"That's because Amy isn't a French name, so the people who adopted her changed it," Amy told her. "She's the only one with a different name."

"What about your friend, the one who was with us last night?" Aimee asked. "You called her something different, didn't you?"

Amy didn't want anyone using the word *different* about Aly. "It was a nickname, that's all. She's an Amy too, just like us. She's Number Three." She hoped Aly wasn't having any problems remembering her number. The counting off of teams had resulted in her being with Number Five—and Amy definitely didn't want Five having any doubts about Aly.

"And you've got a number too," Eleven said to Aimee. "Whether you want it or not. You're just like the rest of us. Only snottier."

Amy couldn't blame Eleven for feeling a little hostile toward Aimee. The actress had done nothing but whine and complain since they'd started on their search. And she hadn't really helped at all. Amy and Eleven carried the bags and did most of the gathering. Aimee wouldn't climb trees for nuts (she might scrape her knees). Or bend down for plants (it gave her a backache).

"Well, I don't know my number," Aimee snapped. "So you're just going to have to call me by my name. Or don't speak to me at all."

"Fine with me," Eleven snapped back at her.

Amy rolled her eyes. "You're Number Ten," she told Aimee. "Whether you like it or not."

"Are you sure about that?" Eleven asked. "She acts like a Zero. Aren't you going to help us pick these strawberries?"

Aimee gazed down at them in distaste. "They look dirty. And I don't want to ruin my manicure."

Amy thought that if Eleven's vision had been any stronger, Number Ten would have been stabbed by actual daggers by the time they returned to the clearing. All the clones were chattering as they emptied their bags on long tables that had been set up for them.

"Let's get all the fruit stuff and the plant stuff separated," Five suggested. "We can pile all the nuts in this big shell."

"Good idea!" Aly chirped. "It might help us if we can make it look good, like real food."

Five laughed merrily. "It *is* real food, Three! You should know that better than anyone." To the group in general, she said, "Three was fantastic, she could spot something edible a mile away!"

Amy glanced at Five through narrowed eyes. She couldn't have been speaking literally—there was no way Aly could see a mile away. But Aly was beaming from Five's praise.

"I would have eaten a poison mushroom if it wasn't for her," Five continued. "She stopped me just in time!"

"You shouldn't have been eating anything anyway," Amy said to her. "We're supposed to be working as a team, remember? Not looking out for ourselves."

Immediately, she regretted speaking out. She didn't need to remind Five that they'd been enemies the last time they'd met. Fortunately, Aimee chose that moment to announce that she was on the verge of collapse. "It's so hot here," she moaned. "This island should be air-conditioned."

"It doesn't feel too warm to me," Five declared. "How about the rest of you?"

The others agreed that they felt fine—even Aly, despite the fact that there were beads of perspiration on her forehead. Amy hoped no one else had noticed that.

One of the other girls—Number Two, Amy thought—was studying Aimee. "You're an actress, aren't you? I saw you on TV."

Aimee rewarded the clone with a brief smile. "Yes,

I'm Aimee Evans. My agent told me I was going to be making a new commercial here. I'm going to have him fired as soon as I get back. I don't think I need an agent. I've already got too many people hanging around me. A publicist, a secretary, my hairdresser, my physical trainer, my—"

Two wasn't impressed. "You shouldn't be doing that," she said bluntly. "Going on TV, putting yourself where the public can see you. Trying to become famous."

Aimee sighed dramatically and rolled her eyes. "I'm *already* famous. Besides, it's none of your business. Why shouldn't I be on TV?"

Number Four clearly knew what Two was getting at, and she joined the conversation. "You shouldn't be on TV because you're drawing attention to yourself," she said. "If people find out what you are, what you can do, you could be in trouble."

"And that could end up getting all of us in trouble," another girl chimed in.

Amy agreed with them. Her own mother had stopped her from getting into gymnastic competitions because Amy risked becoming a public figure. But she thought that these girls were forgetting an important fact.

"We're *already* in trouble," Amy pointed out. "We've been captured by our enemies! The people who brought us here, the organization—these are the people we've been hiding from!"

"Who's hiding from who?" That question came from Cindy, who had just arrived in the clearing. She was accompanied by a man Amy thought she recognized. He'd been with the Andys in *their* clearing last night.

Amy tried to come up with a story to back her statement, but Five interceded.

"We were talking about the edible plants. It was hard finding them—it was like they were hiding from us!"

Amy looked at Five suspiciously. Why was this clone protecting her? But Cindy seemed to accept what Five said, and turned her attention to the table.

"You've done well!" she exclaimed. She and the man moved around the table, examining the stuff the girls had brought back, making notes, and weighing the food on a little scale. Amy thought it looked like a lot, but she had no idea how well the boys had done.

Apparently, not as well as the girls did. After a brief consultation, the man strode away and Cindy beamed at the Amys. "We won!"

A cheer went up. Three Amys hugged each other and jumped up and down. Amy tried to conceal her disbelief as she noted their reaction. Were they just faking it for Cindy's benefit? Or were they actually buying into this stupid game?

"We couldn't have done it without *her*," one of the girls said, pointing to Aly. "She knows all about plants and stuff. Hey, what's your number anyway?"

Aly looked at Amy. "Three," Amy said quickly. "You know, Cindy, it's not easy remembering each other, when we all look alike. Couldn't we have T-shirts with our numbers on them?"

"We've got a better plan," Cindy told her. "T-shirts can be exchanged or mixed up. Something more permanent is needed."

Amy waited apprehensively. Surely they wouldn't be branded like cows. No, the plan of the organization was much less painful. Three Pink Smocks silently appeared, carrying bowls and bottles.

"We're going to put streaks in your hair!" Cindy told them. "It's a very hip look. And you'll each have a different color so you'll be able to tell each other apart."

Several clones gave their approval with happy shrieks. "I've always wanted a green streak," someone declared. "But my mother said no."

"Can I have orange?" someone asked. Amys were gathering around the expressionless robot-clones to examine the color choices. Two of them began playfully arguing over a particularly vibrant crimson.

At least Number Eight wasn't joining in the general glee. Once again, she sidled up to Amy and whispered,

"How can they be so *happy*? Don't they realize we're prisoners here?"

"I guess they're starting to feel like this really is a vacation," Amy said. "We're on a gorgeous island, after all. And Cindy's nice to them. They're getting streaks in their hair. They've won the first competition and they won't have to vote anyone off."

"But the other team will," Eight noted. "I wonder how *they're* feeling right now?"

Amy hadn't even considered that—but now, the notion hit her with a thud. What if the Andys voted *her* Andy off the island? Would Andy be gone before she even found him?

And if he was the ejected clone—she didn't even know what would happen to him.

# nine

The sand was soft, silky, and warm. Amy stretched luxuriously and raised her face to catch the sun. In another minute or two, she thought she might join some of her sister clones who were splashing in the ocean and bodysurfing on the big waves.

Immediately, she berated herself for her actions and thoughts. This *wasn't* how she should be feeling—she knew that. It was exactly how Cindy wanted them to feel—loose, easy, relaxed. Not suspicious. It would be so easy to forget, to believe that they were really on a vacation.

She had to resist falling into this trap the organization

had set for them. She tried to feel angry and combative, but it wasn't easy. They were being held prisoner here, against their will—but Amy was beginning to realize just how seductive their jail cell could be. This place was like a fantasy, and it was getting very hard to think of it as a nightmare.

"Could you put some suntan lotion on my back?" Aly asked her.

"Sure," Amy said. She turned to Number Eight. "Have you got the lotion?"

Eight lazily tossed it to her. Amy recognized the tube as that of an expensive brand, the kind her mother used when they went to the beach. The organization was sparing no expense.

"Your skin isn't as vulnerable to the sun as ordinary people's," Cindy had told them. "You're much less likely to get skin cancer or severe burns. But you still need protection. We don't want you to take any health risks. You're much too valuable!" Cindy was always saying stuff like that, making them feel secure and important. Amy had to admire the psychology the woman was using. The organization wasn't made up of dummies—which made them even more dangerous.

Amy applied an extra-thick layer to Aly's back. She knew her friend could burn like any ordinary person, and she didn't want a little redness to give Aly away. Meanwhile, Aly held the lock of blue hair that now decorated her head over her eyes.

"It's kind of cool, isn't it? I mean, when the sun hits it, it really shines."

"It's gorgeous," Eight said sarcastically. She fingered her own pink streak. "Now we're not just clones, we're fashion victims too."

"Let's just hope that's the only kind of victims we are," Amy remarked.

"Oh, you guys are so gloomy," Aly scolded. She gazed out at the others on the beach. "Those girls in the pink smocks did a good job, didn't they? Everyone has a streak in the exact same place."

"That's because the Pink Smocks are practically robots," Amy told her. "They follow orders because they have no individuality, no minds of their own. The organization created those girls to be their slaves, Aly. These are *bad* people. Don't forget that."

"And *you* shouldn't forget to call me Three instead of Aly," Aly reprimanded her. "We're all supposed to be alike here, remember?"

Amy remembered. She just hoped Aly would remember that a number wouldn't really make her like the others. She'd already slipped up once, showing the others that she couldn't do math quickly in her head. Aly couldn't afford mistakes like that. It would be better all around if she just kept her mouth shut.

Fingering her own lock of streaked hair, Amy held it in front of her eyes. Bright purple was one of her favorite colors. Could the organization have known that?

She had to admit, she kind of liked it. Now she looked like a typical teen enjoying the latest fad. Her mother was going to kill her. . . . And then she reminded herself that she'd be lucky if she survived long enough to give her mother that opportunity.

Eight gazed out at the two Pink Smocks who were now sticking poles into the sand. "What are they doing?"

"Setting up a volleyball net," Amy told her.

Aly clapped her hands. "Ooh, I love beach volleyball, don't you?"

"We don't play a lot of beach volleyball in Brooklyn," Eight said. "I think I'll sit this game out."

Aly got up. "C'mon, Amy. I mean, Seven."

"Aly, wait."

"What?"

"Come *here*." Amy beckoned for Aly to come closer so she could speak into her ear. The other girls on the beach had gathered around the net and were choosing teams excitedly, but if their listening skills were as developed as Amy's, she knew they'd be able to hear her.

She whispered. "Aly, these girls are going to play killer volleyball."

"So what?" Aly asked. "I was the best volleyball player at camp last summer."

"Yeah, but you were playing with regular, normal people, remember? Look!"

The clones were taking some practice shots. Five slammed the ball so it flew way beyond the clone on the other side. But the metallic gold–streaked Amy— Number Eleven, Amy was pretty sure—ran backward so fast she was practically a blur, and managed to jump higher than an L.A. Laker on a good day to slam the ball back to the other side.

Aly gaped at them.

"See? You can't do that," Amy told her. "Remember, Aly, you have to keep a low profile. You were lucky with that natural food competition yesterday. It didn't require any extraordinary skills. The next challenge might be a lot harder. You don't want the others to notice that you can't do everything they can do."

Aly understood. "Because if we lose the next challenge, they'd vote me off, because I'd be the weakest member of the team."

Amy nodded. She didn't want to remind Aly that they still didn't know what being voted off really meant. But Aly seemed to believe they were really going to follow the pattern of the TV show.

"I don't want to go home," Aly said. "Not yet. This place is too cool." She looked longingly as the volleyball game went on. "Maybe I'll just move closer, so I can watch." She scampered down the beach.

Eight was looking at her curiously. Amy realized that the clone had probably heard everything.

"What was *that* all about?" she asked.

Amy considered her options and decided she'd have to trust someone with this secret. She might not be able to protect Aly on her own.

"Three isn't like us," she told Eight. "She's not even really Three. Three died in the hospital. Aly was Number Thirteen." She told Eight the story of Aly, how Aly's genetic manipulation had been unsuccessful. She explained how they'd met and become friends, and how she was trying to keep the others from finding out the truth about the thirteenth clone.

"I had a funny feeling about her," Eight admitted. "She's sweet and nice, but kind of, I don't know . . . not very *quick*."

Amy nodded. "So, will you help me keep her safe?"

Eight nodded. "Yeah. We need to start forming our alliance."

"Our what?"

"Didn't you watch *Survivor?*"

Amy shook her head. "I was always forgetting to set the VCR."

"Well, certain team members formed alliances, pledging not to vote each other off. You and me and Three can start an alliance."

Amy agreed. "Should we ask others to join us?"

Eight looked out at the group playing volleyball. "Not Five. I don't trust her."

"Me neither," Amy said. "When we were at the hospital, I caught her talking to that doctor in charge. Did you know she was a spy? She was collaborating with the organization the whole time. She betrayed her own clone sisters."

Eight was horrified. "I knew there was something I didn't like about her. Don't you think we should warn the others?"

"They won't believe us." Amy sighed. "Five's too popular. Just make sure you never tell her anything we're doing or planning. It'll get right back to the organization. And we don't want Ten on our side either."

"The actress?" Eight agreed with Amy. "Yeah, she's

pretty worthless. What about the one with the black streak, Number Nine? She wasn't with us at the hospital, was she?"

"No. She's a French ballerina." Amy told Eight about her encounters with Annie Perrault in Paris. "She's *evil*. She hangs out in the Paris Catacombs with these creepy people who think they're superior to the rest of the world. They want to get rid of everyone who's different from them, or turn them into slaves."

"Wow," Eight commented. "The organization is going to *love* her. Maybe we should use our alliance to vote her off first." She fell silent for a moment. "It's creepy, the idea of voting someone off. We don't know what will happen to that person."

"On *Survivor*, the person just went home, right?"

Eight nodded. "But there's a lot going on here that's different from the TV show. Like, those people were really stranded. They had to make their own shelters, find their own food all the time. . . . It wasn't all nice and comfortable like it is here. So we can't believe that everything will be like it was on television."

Eight was right. And there was something else on Amy's mind. "It doesn't make sense," she said. "Why would they go to all this trouble to bring us together when they're just going to send us home, one after another?"

Eight considered that question. "Maybe . . . maybe they don't *need* all of us. Maybe that's why we have these challenges. To see who's the most perfect."

Amy recalled Cindy's words. "Cindy said we're supposed to be perfect in three ways—physically, intellectually, and emotionally. I guess each competition will test a different type of perfection."

"Mmm." Eight murmured. She was gazing beyond Amy now, and Amy turned to see what she was looking at. Cindy, wearing shorts and a halter top, was coming onto the beach.

"Girls! Gather round, please! It's time for a challenge!"

"What *is* emotional perfection anyway?" Eight wondered as they got up and started toward Cindy.

"I haven't the slightest idea," Amy said. "So I hope *this* challenge isn't going to test it."

# ten 10

From Cindy's description of the next competition, Amy didn't think Aly should have any special problem with this challenge.

"A labyrinth has been created in the woods," Cindy told them. "A maze of paths lined with hedges. There are two entrances, but only one exit. Each team will enter the labyrinth from a different entrance. The objective of the mission is to find your way out within one hour. The team who gets the most members out by the end of the hour wins the challenge."

"But if we're all together, won't we all come out at the same time?" Number Eight asked.

Cindy smiled. "You won't stay together."

"*We'll* stay together," Amy assured Eight and Aly as they headed back to their cabins to change out of their swimsuits. "Us three. No matter what happens, we'll stick together in this maze thing."

"What kind of special talent is this challenge supposed to test?" Eight wondered.

"I'm not sure," Amy admitted. "Having a good sense of direction? Or maybe we have to climb, or jump, or something like that to get through the labyrinth. Don't worry, Aly," she added hastily, "Eight and I will help you."

"Or maybe *this* is a test of our emotional perfection," Eight remarked.

"What's emotional about it?" Aly wanted to know.

"Panic," Eight said. "I saw an experiment once where a bunch of little white rats were put in a maze. They went crazy, not being able to find their way out."

"We're not little white rats," Amy said sharply. But back in her cabin, as she changed her clothes, she wondered if Eight might not be on the right track. This could be what Cindy meant by "emotional perfection"—staying calm if you got lost and confused, not freaking out like the rats did.

It was strange, Amy mused, this notion of emotional perfection. For a long time she had known that she was physically superior to her normal friends. And she knew she was smarter—it was easier for her to learn, and she had practically a photographic memory. But she'd never thought of herself as unique or different in an emotional way. She could feel happy, sad, angry, jealous, just like anyone else.

The girls met back at the clearing, and Cindy led them into the woods. It was about a thirty-minute hike to the labyrinth, and there wasn't much talking among them. Everyone was a little nervous, wondering what this new challenge would be all about.

But Amy—and everyone else—relaxed once they reached the area. The labyrinth didn't look like a place that would make anyone panic. In the bright light of the day, it had the appearance of a manicured park—neat and green and attractive. The high hedge that extended about a quarter of a mile looked perfectly sweet, as if it could conceal a carousel or a children's playground.

Most of the girls were more intrigued by another sight. "The boys!" Number Two squealed, and they all looked down the length of the hedge to the opposite end, where they could just make out twelve identical figures, plus a man. The boys were too far away for any of them to make out details, but one thing was clear—the boys were using the same method as the girls to individualize themselves. There were flashes of red, green, blue, and every other color in the blond hair that crowned each Andy. Amy wondered which color *her* Andy wore.

"Where?" Aly asked. "I don't see any boys."

Amy wasn't standing close enough to Aly to poke or pinch her, and she could only groan silently. Would Aly ever learn to keep her mouth shut?

"Down there, just look!" a clone advised her. Amy noticed that Five was looking at Aly. It made her nervous.

Cindy spoke sternly. "Girls, don't forget, that's the other team over there. Your competition. There should be no fraternizing with the enemy."

"Not *ever?*" Two asked in dismay.

She wasn't the only one who looked disappointed, but Cindy ignored them and lined the girls up in their numerical order. Amy was pleased to have Eight right behind her, and wished that Aly wasn't so far ahead of them. In single file, giggling and still trying to get glimpses of the boys, they marched into the opening in the hedge.

A narrow path between two high hedges greeted them. They walked along for a few yards, until they came upon an open arch in the hedge on their right side. Number One turned into the arch, Number Two followed, and so did Aly. But Four stopped.

"Wait, why are you guys turning?" she wanted to know. "We could just keep going straight."

"Why?" asked Five.

"Because we should continue in the same direction," Four said. "If we start turning, we'll get confused."

"But maybe this is the direction toward the exit," Five said.

Personally, Amy thought going straight made more sense. But since Aly had already turned, she decided she would turn too. Eight followed her, but some of the girls behind Eight kept on the same path with Four. A quick count told Amy that they'd split evenly, six and six. So Cindy had been right—they wouldn't stay together.

Amy's group faced another choice almost immediately, with the option to turn right again. They all followed One into the arch, but everyone stopped when they realized there was a more confusing option now—going straight, or choosing between two arches just a few feet apart on the left side of the hedge.

"Let's keep straight," One said.

"Why?" Two asked.

"I don't know," One said almost irritably. "I mean, it's a risk any way we go. What difference does it make?"

"It's the difference between heading east and turning north," Two pointed out.

"No, that's not true," Five argued. "We started out heading east. But that first arch turned us to the south."

"Are you sure about that?" Eight asked.

"I want to take the second opening on the left," Aly suddenly declared.

"Why?" Amy wanted to know.

"Why not?" Aly countered.

She had a point. All they could really do was try not to go back in the direction they'd come from. All Amy knew was that whatever direction Aly took, she would take that direction too.

So while One and Two kept moving in a straight line, Three, Five, Seven, and Eight turned left at the second arch. In front of them, Five was chattering to Aly. "I don't care what Cindy says, I want to meet those boys! Don't you?"

"Absolutely," Aly said. "Are they really cute?"

Eight whispered into Amy's ear. "We need to get Aly away from Five."

Amy agreed. Not only was she worried about what Five might be thinking about Three, she also knew that it would be best if she and Eight were alone with Aly. If they had to provide Aly with any aid, no one else should be around.

But they had a problem losing Five. Aly was now at the head of the line, and she turned to consult Five at each decision-making juncture. And they always seemed to agree on the direction—which made Amy even more suspicious of Five. Because Aly clearly had no sense of direction, and after a few more twists and turns, Amy felt sure that they were heading back in the direction they'd come from—which couldn't bring them to the exit.

A look at her watch informed her that they had half an hour till the competition was officially over. She supposed that if the other girls found their way out by then, the team could win, if the boys didn't manage to get more of their team out. Still, Amy wanted to be one of the girls who helped her team win.

So did Eight. And when Aly started to turn right for the third time in a row, Eight stopped short. "C'mon, you guys, that's all wrong. We should turn left here."

"No, I think we should go straight," Five declared.

"Well, I'm going left," Amy declared. "Go left, Aly."

She wasn't sure whether Aly had heard her, or if she was just trying to assert herself and do the opposite of what Amy said. Or maybe she was so confused she didn't know the difference between right and left. In any case, Aly didn't turn left, she went right, and Five followed her, even though she'd said they should go straight.

Amy hesitated. "Go left," Eight whispered.

Amy knew Eight was correct, that right was the wrong way to go. But she didn't want to leave Aly alone with Five. Aly was so naïve—if Five was very friendly, Aly just might blurt out the truth about herself. And word would spread rapidly that there was a fake clone among them.

So Amy went right—but she came upon an empty path. Four different arches led away from it, but Amy had no idea which one Aly and Five had taken.

She sighed. "I guess we should go back to the left," she said to Eight, but when she looked over her shoulder, Eight wasn't there. Amy was alone.

She listened, hard, for the sound of other footsteps, but heard nothing. She started walking briskly to the left, but after a few steps her pace faltered. Why didn't this feel right? Had she too lost her sense of direction?

And now the maze didn't seem quite so pretty, or so innocent. There was an eerie silence and a stillness about it that gave her the creeps.

Amy took a few tentative steps and then stopped again. Did she have any idea where she was heading? Surely she should be able to hear someone else. Or see someone else. Maybe if she climbed the hedge . . .

But there was no way to climb it, no limb strong enough to hold her up. She tried jumping, but couldn't get that high.

Now her pulse quickened, and a dark thought hovered in her head. Cindy hadn't said anything about the team members who didn't make it out of the maze. Surely the organization would send a search party to find any lost clones. Or maybe they had a helicopter that would hover above the labyrinth and locate missing people.

Or maybe not. Maybe she'd be left there to—to what? Wander endlessly, aimlessly? How long could a person survive without food or water? Was this just another way that the organization planned on eliminating the clones who weren't the best?

A shiver went through her. Panic . . . that was what she was feeling. So much for emotional perfection.

Then, very faintly, she thought she heard a slight rustling sound. It could be an animal, she supposed. A squirrel . . . a little white rat . . .

But maybe it was a person. And suddenly, Amy felt a desperate desire *not* to be alone. She clenched her fists tightly, squeezed her eyes shut, and focused all her energy and concentration on her hearing. Yes, there it was again, that faint rustle . . . coming from behind her . . .

She turned and ran back the way she came, looking for an opening to the right. . . . There were two; she took the first one but saw nothing. She ran back out and into the second opening. The rustling sound started up again, slightly louder . . . to the left . . . no, farther left . . . then the next turn to the right . . . she stopped.

He stood there, his back to her. She didn't need to see his face to know that he was an Andy.

But which one?

# eleven

He heard her and turned. For a second, he too seemed relieved to not be alone. But in the next second, his expression became wary.

She could relate to that. She felt wary too. She had one chance in twelve of having found herself face to face with someone who wasn't a total stranger.

She supposed it wouldn't be that hard to find out if this was the Andy she knew. All she needed to do was ask a question or two. Like, did we meet at Wilderness Adventure, where we witnessed a murder? Did we climb to the top of the Eiffel Tower in Paris and kiss there?

But what if he wasn't her Andy? What would she be giving away? For all she knew, he could be a clone working with the organization, someone on the side of the enemy—a collaborator, like Number Five. He could be looking for something to use against another member of his team. The past, the knowledge that she and Andy shared . . . as far as she could tell, the organization knew nothing about it. She thought it was best if things stayed that way.

So she and this boy continued to stare at each other uneasily. Amy noticed that the stripe in his hair was purple, and that gave her an idea. It was something to comment on, and he'd have to respond, and maybe they'd recognize each other's voice.

"Your streak is the same color as mine," she said.

"Yeah," he replied. "It is."

*That* told her nothing, and clearly her voice hadn't made any sort of impression on *him,* either.

Should she make reference to a name only *her* Andy would recognize? Like who? One of the other campers at Wilderness Adventure? Or maybe the guy who fell off the Eiffel Tower just before they kissed? Mr. Devon, the mystery man, whose dead body they had both seen behind the wheel of a car in a gas station?

But even if this was *her* Andy, he might not admit to knowing any of them. He could pretend he didn't know her to protect himself. Or to protect *her*.

Then they both heard female voices.

"Look, there's the twig on the hedge that I bent. We *have* turned this way before."

"Then we shall proceed to the left," another voice replied. "I feel certain this is correct."

The second voice had a distinct accent. Amy kept her eyes on the Andy in front of her, and she didn't miss the flash of alarm that crossed his features. He recognized that voice, just as she had.

She took the plunge. "You know her. So do I. From Paris."

"The Catacombs," he whispered. "Amy? Is it really you?"

She nodded. "Andy . . ." She realized as she spoke that they both were being silly. Practically everyone on the island was named Amy or Andy, and acknowledging the names didn't mean a thing.

But that didn't matter, nothing mattered. Not being trapped on an island or lost in a labyrinth. Andy, the real Andy, was there. Not that she expected him to rescue her, or make everything okay. But at least she wasn't alone—there was someone she could absolutely positively count on, someone who had been in life-or-death situations with her, someone who cared.

He had to be thinking this too, she thought. And just like her, he probably wanted to hug, kiss, do something to express what they were both feeling. But something about the moment kept them both uncertain.

"It's good to see you," he said awkwardly.

"It's good to see you, too," she echoed. Then they both grinned, recognizing the irony in the comments. There were eleven other people on the island who looked exactly like him, and eleven who were identical to her. Why would "seeing" each other be special?

But it was. And Amy knew why. It was because they knew each other in a way the others didn't and couldn't. She and Andy had been through too much together.

He took a step toward her, but then stopped. Amy had picked up on the sound of footsteps too. A second later, a boy with Andy's blue eyes appeared through an opening. He spoke to Andy.

"You been down that way?" He pointed to the opening on the other side, just beyond Amy.

"No," Andy said. "But it feels like the right direction."

The other Andy glanced suspiciously at Amy, then back at his replica. "You coming? We've only got about fifteen minutes."

"Yeah. I'll follow you." Andy let the boy pass; then he muttered something in Amy's ear before hurrying to catch up with his clone. He spoke rapidly and very softly, but Amy got the message.

"Ten o'clock. By the coral reef on the rocky beach."

Then he was gone.

# twelve 12

Maybe it was seeing Andy that calmed her panic and got her focused again. In any case, she felt stronger and surer, and her hearing seemed to have become more acute. She was ready to move on, and she had a renewed sense of direction.

Without further hesitation, she took off down the path that the two Andys had taken. Seconds later, another Amy appeared on the same path, and they soon found themselves behind two more. All the girls began walking faster, and it wasn't much longer before a slight gust of a breeze told them they were nearing an exit. Sighs of relief swept down the line of clones, and

Amy had a feeling they were all going to emerge from the maze singing "Ninety-nine Bottles of Beer on the Wall" or some other silly camp song.

They didn't sing—but they burst out of the labyrinth giggling like maniacs. The Amys who had already emerged burst into cheers, and the Andys—who had gathered a safe distance from the girls—were counting them.

Number One gave her the update. "They're leading. We've got seven out now, they've got nine."

"Four minutes, thirty seconds," the man who was in charge of the Andys called out. Everyone's eyes were on the exit.

Aimee Evans limped out. "Look at my shoes," she wailed. "They're ruined!"

Sure enough, her strappy sandals weren't in very good shape. "Why didn't you wear the running shoes we gave you?" Cindy wanted to know.

"They're ugly," Aimee whined.

The man declared the time every thirty seconds. At first, everyone was excited, watching the exit and waiting to see who would come out next. But when there was only one minute left and no one else had emerged, the mood swiftly changed.

Amy went to Cindy. "What happens if someone is lost inside the labyrinth? How do we get them out?"

"That's not for you to worry about," Cindy said.

The answer wasn't satisfying. "Well, is *someone* worrying about it?" Amy persisted.

Cindy looked at her calmly. "Seven, any clone who can't find her way out of the labyrinth doesn't deserve to be among the elite."

Was she saying what Amy *thought* she was saying? She gasped, but Cindy simply turned back to the exit and smiled. Three more Amys came running out.

"Thirty seconds," the man called.

"We're going to win!" Number Five shrieked excitedly.

Amy did a rapid survey of hair streaks. Yellow, crimson, light green, lavender, Kelly green, white, black, orange, pastel pink, hot pink—no blue. No Aly. A sound of footsteps—but it turned out to be an Andy.

"Number Three is missing!" she cried out to Five. She had a vision of poor, frightened Aly, somewhere in the labyrinth, alone and running in circles.

"But now we've got eleven and they've got nine," Five replied. "We've got the lead!"

"Fifteen seconds," the man called.

Amy couldn't stand the thought of Aly lost in that maze of hedges. She had to do something. "Seven, where are you going?" she heard someone yell, and then others were calling too, but she ignored the shrill, angry voices that followed her as she ran back into the labyrinth.

"Aly!" she yelled as she raced down a path. "Aly, can you hear me?" And at every arch, she stuck her head through the opening and called her lost clone's name. "Aly, where are you?" Everyone outside the labyrinth could probably hear her, and she knew she should be using Aly's number and calling for Three, but Aly was more likely to respond to her own name.

And sure enough, Amy did hear something—a voice without a lot of power. The caller was mustering all the strength she had to scream, "Here! I'm here!"

"Keep yelling, don't stop!" Amy shouted. She was able to follow the cries, down one path, up another, knowing she was getting closer. And then she found Aly, huddled in a little heap on the ground, looking totally frightened.

Amy helped her up, gave her a quick hug, then hustled her back the way she'd come. But when they emerged from the labyrinth, there were no cheers. The Andys were nowhere to be seen, and the Amys were glaring at Amy and Aly.

"The last two boys came out," Eight told Amy. "So they won."

"I thought they only had nine out," Amy said. "What about their last one?"

"They only have eleven," Eight said. "One got voted

off the island last night, because they lost the natural food challenge."

Amy had forgotten about the losing team's punishment. And now Cindy was telling them that they'd be facing the same ordeal.

The woman wasn't smiling as she gave them their instructions. "You will each go back to your own cabin and stay there until the sun goes down. Then we will meet at the clearing. You can spend the time thinking about which team member you can do without."

There was no chance to talk or share opinions. Cindy led the silent line of girls back to the area where the cabins stood. Once inside her own cabin, Amy wasn't inclined to seek out anyone else—and she felt very sure no one would be coming to see her.

So now it was a question of who the others were angrier at—her or Aly. She could count on Eight not to vote off either of them, but it was too bad there hadn't been time to get more people into their alliance before this happened. The others would consider the weakest team member to be her or Aly. One of them would be banished. Going home.

Then Amy realized something. Even if the rejected team member was truly sent safely home, she still didn't want to be that person. Not because this island was such a lovely vacation paradise, but because something was going on here, and she had to find out what it was. It could be just what Cindy told them—a chance for the organization to assess their progress. But why? What did the organization really want from them?

These were questions that had tortured her from the beginning, or at least from the time she'd first learned what she was. The clones couldn't be simply an interesting scientific experiment. Too much secrecy and expense had gone into their making. Someone had plans for them, big plans. Here, with both sets of clones present, there was a chance of finding out what those plans were. Amy intended to find out.

Was there anything she could do to keep the others from voting her off? Was there anything she could bribe them with, threaten them with? Was there some way, in the next couple of hours, that she could become the most popular girl on the island?

It didn't look like it. All Amy could do was hope the other Amys liked someone else even less than her. Only, she also hoped that person wouldn't be Aly . . . or Eight.

As the sun began to set, there was the sound of a bell. She'd heard the same ringing the night before, but hadn't known what it meant. Now she suspected it was the call to the clearing.

She came out of her cabin as the other girls came out of theirs. As if by some signal, they all started toward the clearing. No one spoke. Maybe that was why their footsteps on the dirt path seemed louder and echoed in the still night.

The clearing had been transformed. It wasn't the cheerful picnic grounds of just a few hours earlier. Now, tall burning lanterns cast an ominous glow over the gray rocks. Cindy was there to greet them, but she wasn't smiling. And she wasn't alone.

There were two men with her. One of them might have been the guy who led the Andys—he seemed about the same height and build. But Amy wouldn't have been able to recognize him. Both men had their faces covered with black ski masks. If that wasn't enough to make them scary, their clothes—military camouflage shirts and pants—lent more creepiness to their appearance. Amy told herself this was all for dramatic effect—to freak them out—but she wasn't so sure. And she wished she could tell Aly that too. Number Three was white with fear.

Cindy motioned for the girls to take seats on the rocks. Then she spoke in clear, measured tones.

"This is where you must make a painful decision," she told them solemnly. "You have to lose one of your team members. This will be difficult for you. You may have become friends over the past two days. You may even think of yourselves as sisters. But more than anything else, you have to be a team, united, joined together like a chain—and a chain is only as strong as its weakest link. Tonight, you must discard that weak link."

Amy could feel the chill of Cindy's words pass like a shiver down the row of girls. No one spoke—no one even seemed to be breathing.

Cindy explained the procedure. One by one, the girls would go down the path into the woods. There, they would find a table on which lay a bowl, papers, and a pencil. Each would write down the number of the girl whom she was voting off the island.

Amy let her eyes stray to Eight. If only there was some way that they could exchange a message! If every girl voted for a different Amy, then two votes for the same person could have an impact. They would absolutely have to get their alliance pulled together and their votes synchronized in the next go-round. If they both survived this night.

They went to cast their votes in numerical order. When it was Amy's turn, she found herself in a state of complete confusion. She still had no idea whom she was going to vote for.

If she followed Cindy's instructions and voted off

the weakest member, she knew without a doubt who that would be—Aly. And if she believed that the rejected member was sent home, she wouldn't have had a problem with that. But there was no way she'd vote for Aly when she didn't know what the consequences for Aly would be.

So she decided to vote for the girl she thought was the most dangerous. But even then, it was hard to make a decision. Two clones fit the bill: Amy, Number Five, who supported the organization and encouraged the other girls to be on her side, and Annie Perrault, or Amy, Number Nine, who was a truly evil person.

She knew more about Nine, so maybe she was better equipped to fight her. She scrawled the number five on her paper and put it in the bowl.

Finally all the girls had taken the walk into the woods and voted. The two masked men brought the bowl to Cindy, who took out the papers one at a time, looking at each carefully. When she finished, she looked up solemnly.

"Number Ten."

For a moment, Amy was puzzled. Which one was ten? Then she remembered. It was Aimee Evans. Obviously, the actress's whining and complaining had gotten on more nerves than her own.

Aimee clearly didn't have any problem with the

decision. "That's just fine with me," she snapped, standing up. "But if I don't get that sitcom because of this delay, I'm going to sue. Where's the boat? How do I get home?"

The silent masked men were now standing on either side of her. They weren't holding her, or even touching her, just accompanying her away from the clearing. Aimee didn't seem to be anyone's prisoner.

And yet, Amy had the sinking suspicion that if Number Ten were to make a run for it, right then and there, she wouldn't get very far.

# thirteen 13

Amy didn't think she would have too much trouble finding the place where she was supposed to meet Andy. The island wasn't that big, and she could eliminate the beach closest to the girls' cabins, since there was no coral reef there. She would just go around the shoreline and look.

What she hadn't counted on was finding another Amy sneaking out of a cabin at the same time she was leaving hers. They were both surprised to see each other.

The yellow-streaked Amy, Number One, spoke first. "What are you doing?"

"I'm going for a walk," Amy replied quickly. "I couldn't

sleep." It sounded fake, but she couldn't come up with anything more convincing. "What are *you* doing?"

"Taking a walk," One said, but she didn't sound any more natural than Amy had.

Amy tried to look nonchalant as One kept pace with her, and they both headed down to the beach. She was pretty sure One had been among the group at the New York hospital, but she couldn't recall having had any clear impressions of her during that time.

"It's a nice night," Amy ventured.

"Yes," One said. "Sort of, I don't know, romantic."

Amy glanced at her sharply. Could One know about her plans with Andy? She supposed it was possible that the girl had overheard them in the labyrinth. Was she planning to stick by Amy's side, to prevent any real meeting or any significant conversation from taking place?

They walked along the shore together. Every time Amy sneaked a peek at One, she realized that One was taking peeks at *her*. Amy was certain they were having identical thoughts. The air around them was thick with distrust.

Then, out of the corner of her eye, Amy glimpsed blond hair around the bend in the shoreline. The coral reef must be around there somewhere. Now if only she could shake off the other girl.

Andy was standing on a pier, his back to them, looking out in the opposite direction. He must have heard footsteps, because he turned around with a big smile on his face. But the smile disappeared when he realized that the girl he was waiting for wasn't alone.

Amy was disappointed too. Ever since knowing the boys were on the island, she'd been waiting for this moment, for the time when they could be together, alone, to talk and plan and . . . kiss. But it wasn't going to happen tonight, not with One right here by her side. She wouldn't be touching Andy's cheek, or running her fingers through his hair, with its green streak . . . wait a minute. *Her* Andy's streak was the same color as hers—purple.

That was when she noticed the disappointment on the face of Number One. And it hit her.

"Are you meeting him?" she asked One point-blank.

One was clearly nervous. "Don't tell Cindy, okay?" she pleaded. "I don't think we're supposed to do this. I mean, they're the enemy, right?"

"I'm not so sure about that," Amy murmured, but this wasn't really the time to discuss the boy clones.

"We met in the labyrinth," One confided in her. "He's Andy Eleven. You won't tell anyone, will you?"

Amy shook her head. "I won't tell. Hey, would you like to be part of an alliance?"

"What kind of alliance?"

"It's me, Three, and Eight, so far. We're all going to vote together when we have to kick someone off the island. Want to join up with us?"

"Sure," One said promptly. Maybe she thought it was the price she had to pay for Amy's silence. In any case, she seemed happy to pay it. Or maybe she just wanted Amy to move on. From the way Amy One and Andy Eleven were looking at each other, Amy could tell that three was a crowd.

So she hurried along, in search of her own Andy. And she found him, where he'd said he'd be—just beyond the coral reef.

She didn't see him right away. Standing uncertainly by the reef, she called softly. "Andy?"

"Over here!"

She followed the reef down a slope, where a mass of stone rose from the beach. There, hidden behind a thick patch of wavy rushes, was a grotto, a small cave cut into the stone. Andy was inside—the right Andy this time, the Andy with the purple streak in his hair.

Suddenly Amy felt shy. It had been a while since that moment on top of the Eiffel Tower. But when he took her hand, all the months and miles that had separated them seemed to disappear. For a few moments, they huddled together silently, relishing the sensation of not being alone.

And it was cozy in the grotto. Despite the fact that they were close to the water, it was bone-dry in there. There were cracks and crevices in the stone, and tiny wildflowers were growing out of them. Andy had brought a candle, and its flickering flame provided just enough light for them to be able to look at each other.

Amy spoke first. "Do you know what's going on here?"

"No," Andy said. "But I think it's big. There are a lot of them around."

She knew he meant organization people. "Where?"

"In a building, on the east end of the island. I went out late last night to look around. I heard voices inside, but the only people I saw were a couple of girls in pink smocks. Do you know who they are?"

"Clones without any will," Amy told him. "They were an early experiment. The organization uses them as slaves. What about the guys with the ski masks? Do you know anything about them?"

He shook his head. "I've seen them around, but they never speak. I guess they could be the male version of the pink-smock girls. Come on, I'll show you the building, and maybe we can get a look inside."

They paused at the entrance to the grotto, but they couldn't hear or see anyone else around.

"How did they get you here?" Amy wanted to know as they made their way up the beach.

He grimaced, as if embarrassed to tell her. "I was tricked. I got this invitation to go on a cruise. It turned out to be a cruise for one."

Amy wondered who he had thought was inviting him—a girl, maybe? She didn't ask.

"What about you?" he asked.

"A—a friend invited me on a boat ride. Only the friend wasn't there."

She'd managed to avoid letting him know that her "friend" was a boy. Not that it really made any difference. It wasn't like she and Andy were girlfriend and boyfriend. She didn't really know how she would classify their relationship. It wasn't a normal romance—but then, they weren't normal people.

The building Andy brought her to was a long, low one-story structure, with a water tank on one end of the roof. It didn't look like anything much was going on there tonight. She saw a glimmer of dim light behind some closed window shades, but no sign of movement.

"Let's try to get inside," Andy whispered.

Amy half expected to see men in camouflage and girls in pink smocks guarding the building, but the grounds were deserted. There was no fence surrounding the place, and no alarms went off as they approached a window.

Andy was a good six inches taller than she was, but

he was still a few inches short. So he held out a hand, Amy put a foot in it, and he hoisted her upward.

She tugged at the sill, but the window didn't budge. And a shade obscured any view of the interior.

It wasn't a thick shade, though. If someone was inside the room, Amy felt sure she would be able to make out a shadow moving.

"Can you see anything?" Andy asked. He was balancing her on his shoulders now.

"No, not yet," Amy said. She concentrated for a while and, to her delight, some images began to form. Shelves on a wall. A desk, with something on it—a computer, maybe. Yes, definitely a computer. Other pieces of machinery . . . a fax machine, a photocopier. Two long narrow tables . . . like operating tables in a hospital. Something was laid out on each of the tables.

Or *someone*? She thought she could see the outlines of limbs, arms and legs, but they were obscured by a sheet.

She tensed up. Those were definitely bodies on the tables. Dead bodies. That was why they were covered with sheets.

Andy must have felt her tension on his shoulders. "What? What do you see?"

But there was no chance to tell him. Two real live figures were coming toward them.

"What are you two doing out here?"

She recognized Cindy's voice and jumped down from Andy's shoulders.

"I was taking a walk," Andy said. "And I saw this girl . . . I guess she's one of the Amys. We started talking, and then we were looking for a place where we could, you know . . ."

Amy kept her face down, hoping she seemed embarrassed, as if they'd just been caught making out. The person who was with Cindy didn't say anything, but just by studying his feet, Amy could see that he was wearing camouflage.

"Well, you shouldn't be together," Cindy said sternly. "We have not authorized any interaction between the two teams. You should both be asleep. In your own cabins. Come along, Seven."

The camouflage man remained silent as he put a hand on Andy's arm and steered him away. Amy heard Andy draw in his breath sharply, and she looked up to see what had surprised him.

There was no ski mask on the man's face. Even in the darkness, Amy had no difficulty making out his features. And recognizing him.

She felt faint, like she'd seen a ghost. The man gave no sign of recognition, but that didn't matter. She knew who he was—she had never forgotten that face.

The man leading Andy away was Mr. Devon.

# fourteen

# 14

A my tossed and turned in her bed that night. Mr. Devon was dead. She knew this for sure. She'd seen his body slumped behind the wheel of a car in a gas station, just after she and Andy had run away from Wilderness Adventure. Mr. Devon had been killed.

But the man she'd seen tonight *was* Mr. Devon. She knew his face well. He had been an assistant principal at her middle school . . . a doctor in a hospital . . . a makeup artist on a movie set. He'd played so many roles in her life . . . watched her, steered her in the right directions, saved her when she landed in the wrong places. She'd never been completely sure who he worked for, where he came from, but she'd felt sure he was on her side. And when she found his body, she believed he'd been killed by the organization.

Yet now he was here, alive. And working with the organization. Had he switched sides? Were they holding him captive, like the Amys and the Andys? It made no sense, no sense at all.

Amy wished she could talk to Andy in the morning. But she didn't dare go searching for him in broad daylight. If she was lucky, she'd run into him during the next challenge, whatever it was. Meanwhile, she could tell Eight, and Aly. And maybe the new member of the alliance, One.

But when she got together with them at breakfast in the clearing, there was something else she had to tell them first—what she'd seen through the window of the organization building.

"Bodies, two of them. Lying on stretchers."

Aly's voice quavered. "Human bodies?"

"Covered with sheets," Amy said. "But I could see that they were human from the way the sheets lay on them."

"You saw all that through the window shade?" Aly was skeptical.

Amy nodded, but Aly wasn't convinced—or maybe she just didn't want to believe her.

"Are you sure you weren't imagining it? How could you see inside the room if the window was covered?"

Eight was getting annoyed with Aly's questions. "Look, you're just going to have to accept what we tell you, okay? We can't waste time explaining everything to you."

But Amy tried. "If something isn't completely opaque, we can see through it if we really focus. Just like we can hear what other people can't if we concentrate hard enough."

"Oh." Aly frowned. "You guys are so lucky. I wish I could do that. It's not fair, I'm supposed to be a clone too."

Eight rolled her eyes in exasperation and turned to Amy. "But you couldn't make out the faces, right?"

"No."

"And there were two of them," Eight mused. Her eyes widened. "Two clones have been voted off the island. An Andy after the first challenge, the actress after the second one."

Amy had been thinking the same thing, but hadn't wanted to say it in front of Aly. Now Aly went pale. "You think—you think they don't send us home if we're voted off? They *kill* us? Ohmigod, Amy, what am I going to do? I can't keep faking it forever, the other clones are going to find out I'm not like you, and I'll be the next one to go!"

"No, you won't," Amy said firmly, and hoped she sounded more sure of herself than she really felt. "We'll win the challenges, so we don't have to vote anyone off."

"But what if we *don't* win?" Aly moaned.

Eight was getting seriously irritated, that was clear. "Stop it," she snapped at Aly. "Don't whine, we'll figure something out."

"I wasn't whining," Aly said, pouting, but Eight ignored her. Her forehead was puckered as she watched Five, who was eating her breakfast with Number Twelve and Annie Perrault, Number Nine.

"Something's going on between those three," Eight said abruptly. "Check out how they whisper, then all look at one girl. I think they're forming an alliance and deciding who they want to vote off."

"Well, we've got our own alliance," Amy reminded her. "And we've got a new member." She looked around and waved to One, who came over and joined them.

"Girls," Cindy called. "Gather round, it's time for a challenge!"

"Quick," Amy said urgently to her alliance. "If we lose this one, we vote off Five, okay?"

"Why her?" Aly wanted to know.

"Just do like we tell you to do," Eight ordered her. Aly looked a little hurt by Eight's tone, but there was no time for Amy to explain more. Cindy was telling them about the challenge.

"It's a scavenger hunt," she announced. "Each of you will be provided with a list of items that have been hidden on the island. The other team will receive the same list. Whichever team brings back the most items in three hours wins the challenge."

She distributed the lists and the bags they had used to gather natural foods. Amy scanned the list quickly, and realized what this challenge was all about.

"It's a test of our vision skills," she said. "All the objects are small. A key, a marble, a safety pin . . ."

Aly was alarmed. "She expects us to find a safety pin in the woods?"

"It's not that hard," One said, studying the list. "Something made of metal gleams. With our eyesight we won't have trouble spotting it if it's hidden in dirt and leaves. Of course, a pin would be harder to find on the beach, since the sand sparkles. We might have to strain a little."

Of course, One didn't know that no amount of strain would ever get Aly's eyes into a condition capable of spotting a safety pin on the beach. Amy squeezed Aly's hand. "Just stay with us," she whispered.

Fortunately, they were allowed to move around the island in groups if they wanted to. Amy's alliance stayed together and started their search in the woods.

They were doing pretty well. Amy found two items from the list—a quarter and a gold locket. Eight did better, spotting the hard-boiled egg, manicure scissors, and a spool of green thread. One got the paper clip and a golf ball.

One spotted something else, too. "Ooh, it's an Andy!" she declared excitedly. "Is he mine?" Her voice fell. "No, he's got a pink streak. He looks like he's coming this way."

"Actually, I wouldn't mind meeting one of those Andys," Eight said casually.

But whatever number this Andy was, he wasn't at all interested in meeting any of them. He strode past without acknowledging them—even shoving Eight in the process.

"Hey!" Eight cried in outrage. "Where are your manners? You ever heard of 'excuse me'?"

But the boy just kept on walking. "They're not all like that," Amy assured her, and One echoed that. They went back to searching for more stuff.

Aly just moaned a lot. "How did you *see* that?" she kept saying over and over, even though she knew perfectly well how extraordinary their eyes were. "I'm never going to find anything," she moaned.

Amy was about to tell her not to worry, that they'd share the stuff they'd found so it would look like Aly had found some of it too, when Eight lost her temper. "Look, will you shut up and stop complaining? You're beginning to get on my nerves."

Aly's eyes filled with tears. Amy put an arm around her, and Eight immediately apologized. "I'm sorry, it's just me and my big mouth," she said. "I'm from New York, and everyone knows people from New York don't have any patience. Especially people from Brooklyn."

Aly didn't seem particularly mollified. And just then, they ran into the other alliance.

"Hi!" Five said brightly. "You guys finding a lot of stuff?" Twelve and Nine were with her.

"Plenty," Eight told her.

"Except for me," Aly said sadly. "I'm no good at this at all."

"Come with us, Three!" Five invited her. "We know all sorts of tricks for finding stuff. We'll teach you."

Aly brightened. "You will?"

*"Aly,"* Amy whispered harshly, but apparently Five's friendliness was a lot more appealing to Aly than Eight's impatience. Aly moved toward them, and before Amy

could say anything more, Five and Nine had their arms around Aly and were leading her away.

Amy frowned. "We've got to get Five out of here. She's too good at making friends."

Eight agreed. "That's why we three have to vote against her." One said she'd try to get Four to align with them.

But they didn't lose the scavenger hunt challenge. It turned out that the Amys located more items from the list than the Andys. They didn't vote anyone off—but the boys would have to do this, and Amy worried again that the boy voted off would be her Andy.

After getting caught last night, she hoped she wouldn't find guards lingering around her cabin that evening. She opened her door carefully and slowly, keeping a vigilant eye out for ski-masked guys in camouflage and pink-smocked girls. She didn't see any. But all the way to the beach, she tried to move silently and keep in the shadows.

As she approached the coral reef, she realized she didn't even know if Andy would be there—they'd been separated so abruptly last night, they hadn't said anything about meeting again. But somehow, she knew that if he was all right, he'd be there. Already, she was thinking of the grotto as "their" place.

And she was right. He was waiting for her inside, sitting on the ground against the wall of the cave. Once again, there was a candle burning, but personally she thought his smile did a better job of lighting up the cavern.

"Did you get in trouble last night?" he wanted to know.

"No. Cindy just walked me back to my cabin. What about you?"

"Same thing."

"Andy . . . you recognized that man, didn't you?"

Andy didn't say anything.

"It was Mr. Devon, Andy."

"Devon's dead," Andy said abruptly. "We both saw him, on the highway outside Wilderness Adventure."

"He *looked* dead," Amy corrected him. "But there wasn't any blood, remember? No bullet holes or wounds, or anything like that. We could have been wrong."

"He was dead," Andy repeated. "Stone-cold dead. Not breathing."

Amy put her hand on his arm gently. "Maybe you just wanted him to be dead."

Andy didn't argue with that. "The man is bad, Amy. He's one of them, he's on their side."

It was an argument they'd had before. Amy shook

her head. "I think you're wrong, Andy. In fact, I'm *sure* you're wrong. He's saved my life."

"He's saved your life to keep you safe for *them*," Andy insisted. "Look, if he isn't dead, if that really was him last night—doesn't that prove my point? He's working for them!"

"Or maybe he's *pretending* to work for them," Amy argued. "He could be a spy, a double agent. I'll bet he's acting like he's on their side so he can keep an eye on us, to make sure they don't hurt us."

"I don't trust him," Andy said stubbornly. "I just don't trust him."

She knew why. Andy had told her back when they first met. He claimed that Mr. Devon had kidnapped him when he was very young and put him in a hospital, where experiments were performed on him.

Amy could associate hospitals with Devon too. She thought she had seen him in that hospital in New York . . . but she'd never been sure. It was all part of the mystery that was Mr. Devon. Maybe someday she'd discover who he really was.

But right now, there were more urgent matters at hand. "Those bodies we saw last night," she said. "Do you really think they could be the clones who were voted off the island?"

"If they are, there'll be three tonight," Andy said.

"We voted off our Number Six earlier. He's been trying to take charge of everything, ordering everyone around. People were sick of him." Andy sighed. "But I don't think any of us wanted him dead."

"We've got to find out," Amy said. "If they're killing us off, we need to tell everyone. *That* should pull them out of this holiday trance they're in."

Andy nodded. "We're going to have to get into that building."

Amy figured out how as they neared the organization building; a ski-masked guy was outside the door, apparently guarding it. Then she heard footsteps, and she pulled Andy down to crouch behind a tree with her. The footsteps belonged to two girls in pink smocks.

"How many of them are there, anyway?" Andy wondered.

"I don't know," Amy said. "But all we need are two." She wasn't sure if it would work. It was possible that the Pink Smocks were programmed to listen only to certain people. But it was worth a try.

She got up and went to them. "Hi, can I borrow your smocks?" she asked. They walked right past her without acknowledging her existence.

She realized she'd taken the wrong approach. The Pink Smocks followed orders, not requests. "Stop!" Amy declared.

The two girls froze.

"Give me your smocks."

A second later she was putting a smock on. "I'm guessing that the guy with the ski mask won't know my face in the dark. He'll think I'm one of the Pink Smocks and let me in. Then I'll go around to the room where we saw the bodies and open the window for you."

She helped Andy into the other—too-tight—smock. "What do I need to wear this for?" he asked.

"If we move really fast, we'll be a blur to normal eyes," she told him. "If the guard sees you going around to the window, he'll just see a flash of pink and won't bother with you."

She thought it was a pretty good plan, but she was still somewhat amazed when it worked. She approached the guard looking straight ahead, her face expressionless. He opened the door.

It dawned on her that it just might be Mr. Devon behind the mask. He'd been wearing those same camouflage clothes last night. She had a sudden impulse to wink, or grin, but she didn't. If he wasn't Mr. Devon, that would be a dead giveaway. She seriously doubted that the Pink Smocks ever winked or grinned.

Once inside, Amy made her way directly to the room where they'd seen the bodies on the stretchers.

Another masked and camouflaged man passed her, but he didn't stop or say anything. This was a piece of cake.

The door to the room wasn't even locked. When she went inside, she saw the covered bodies on the stretchers. Still just two of them. Maybe they weren't too late to save the Andy who had been voted off that evening.

She went to the window, but had to climb on a chair to get it open. Andy was able to leap up to the sill, swing his legs over, and drop down inside.

"Have you looked?" he asked her.

"No. I was waiting for you."

Would he think she was a wimp, not wanting to look at a dead person on her own? No, he seemed to understand perfectly. He took her hand, and they proceeded to the closest stretcher. Carefully he took a corner of the sheet and pulled it up, revealing a face.

The face of Mr. Devon.

Amy squeezed Andy's hand. "You see? He was a spy, he was protecting us, they found out, and they killed him!"

"He's not dead, Amy." Andy pointed, and she noticed the slight rise and fall of Mr. Devon's chest.

"He's sleeping, or drugged, or unconscious in some special way," Andy continued. "But he's not dead."

"Then why was his face covered?" Amy wondered.

"I don't know."

There was still another body to identify. This time Amy took the sheet and pulled it away from the face.

She drew her breath in, and heard Andy gasp at the same time. "Mr. Devon," she whispered. "Another Mr. Devon."

"Clones," Andy said dully. "Just like us."

# fifteen

A couple of days later, at ten o'clock in the evening, Amy was the first to arrive at the grotto. She lit the candle, slumped down to the ground, leaned against the cavern wall, and waited for Andy. The cavern felt cold and bare. She knew it would be cozy and romantic when Andy got there, so she didn't let the atmosphere bother her. Besides, she could always use the time alone to think, to try to put pieces of the puzzle together.

Were all the ski-masked men Mr. Devon clones? Each one was about the same size, but she hadn't seen any of the others' faces. And what kind of clones were they? Were they like the Pink Smocks, with no minds of their own? Or were they like the Amys and Andys, real and human and able to feel? The Mr. Devon whom she had known—was he the original? Or just another replica?

And what had become of the team members who had been voted off the island? Were they back in their own homes? Or at the bottom of the ocean? And what was the point of all these challenges anyway?

There had been a strength competition, where the teams had to lift and carry piles of logs that got heavier and heavier. No one was surprised when the girls lost that one. The boys were older and bigger, and therefore stronger. Amy, Number Four, had been voted off—not because she was weak, but because she kept saying she was homesick.

Then came rope climbing, which had seemed to be a test of agility. The girls should have won that challenge, but Number Twelve slipped, and as two others tried to help her, they all ended up falling. Cindy was annoyed, saying they should have just let Twelve go. They lost, and Twelve was voted off the island.

On the evenings after those competitions, Andy had sat here in the grotto and worried that Amy might have been voted off. But today, the girls triumphed. The challenge was a written exam—states and capitals, some math problems, stuff like that. Now it was Amy's turn to worry.

When she saw him approach, she let out a sigh of relief. But when he bent down to get into the cave, the light from the candle struck his hair. The streak was blue. He wasn't her Andy.

"You're Number Seven, right?" he asked.

She nodded.

"You're supposed to meet Five here?"

It dawned on her that she'd never known Andy's number. He was a person; it was just too impossible to think of him as a digit. Suddenly, she felt sick. "Purple streak," she said faintly.

"Yeah," the boy said. "He's not coming. He was voted off tonight."

Amy pressed a hand against the wall to steady herself. The boy could see her distress. "Wow, you guys must've been getting it on big-time, huh?" He stepped deeper into the cave. "Well, I'm here, babe. Want to hang out?"

"Beat it," Amy said automatically.

He wasn't terribly offended. "Hey, no biggie, there's plenty more like you." And he withdrew from the cave.

Amy remained where she was. She took deep breaths, trying to steady her nerves and think clearly. Of all the puzzle pieces lying around in her head, one stood out from all the others now. One question had a more urgent need to be answered. She couldn't worry about Mr. Devon, or Aly, or the ultimate goals of the organization. She had to know what happened to the clones who were voted off their teams.

She would search the island from end to end. She would climb the highest tree to see as far as possible. She would explore every cave, search for tunnels. She would get into that building again and check out every room.

All this would take time. Too much time, at least on her own. She needed help. Her alliance—Eight, One, even Aly could be given a search assignment.

Amy's mind raced with her legs as she ran back to the cabins. Could she stir up the Amys and Andys and start a revolution? Were they getting sick of their vacation yet? Maybe she could tackle Cindy, threaten to break some bones if the woman didn't tell her where Andy and the others were. Did Cindy have any super-powers? Amy didn't think so. . . . Ideas, plans, possible actions floated through her mind.

And they all came crashing down when she reached the girls' cabins. There would be no revolution tonight. A party was starting up.

At least half a dozen Andys had gathered in front of

the cabins. They were hooting and calling for the girls to come out. And girls were responding.

"We're going down to the beach for a midnight swim," one of the boys was yelling.

An Amy called, "Wait, let me put on my bathing suit."

"We're not going to wear bathing suits!" an Andy called back. Shrieks and giggles came from the cabins.

Surely Eight wouldn't be tempted by this, Amy thought, and started toward the New Yorker's cabin. But she'd forgotten how Eight had been talking just the other day about how she wouldn't mind finding an Andy of her own. . . . Sure enough, her door was open and she was already talking to one of the boys. It seemed like all the other Amys were ready to party with the Andys.

Then a bell rang. It was the bell that called them to the clearing, only this time it clanged in a different rhythm, rapidly, and even more loudly than usual. From out of nowhere, it seemed, men in ski masks and camouflage uniforms appeared—ten, twelve, thirteen, Amy lost count.

They took firm grips on the boys' arms and dragged them away. A few let out feeble protests, but there was no point—these men were stronger. The girls were ushered back into their cabins. Cindy fluttered around among the men, wringing her hands and looking completely exasperated.

"This is exactly what I've been talking about," Amy heard her saying. "Such immature behavior! You are all so far from achieving emotional perfection."

Amy felt a hand latch on to her own arm. Without much hope, she looked plaintively into the ski-masked face. "Mr. Devon? Is that you?" There was no response.

Then she was inside her cabin, alone. From the window, she saw Cindy giving instructions to the men who were left. They took up positions, and it was clear to Amy that she wouldn't be searching the island that night.

She would have to find another way to get herself to where Andy was. And there was only one other way.

# sixteen
# 16

"Today's challenge," Cindy announced the next afternoon, "is a swimming relay."

"Ugh, gross." Eight groaned. "Not *swimming*."

Amy looked at her in alarm. "You don't know how to swim?"

"Oh, I know *how*," Eight said. "I just hate swimming."

"Well, try to do your best," Amy murmured. "But if we do lose, vote against me."

Eight gaped at her. "What!"

This was definitely ironic. Amy was encouraging Eight to swim well, and at the same time, she wanted the girls to lose. But she didn't want Eight to be held responsible for their loss. *She,* Number Seven, wanted to be considered the worst swimmer on the team.

As Cindy went on to explain the relay format, Amy contemplated her own plans for the day. She would get herself voted off the island. That way she'd be able to find out what had happened to all the others. She and Andy would be together, they could start planning and figuring out their next moves. If he was alive . . . but she couldn't think about that now. She had to decide the best way to ensure that the other Amys voted her off.

It couldn't be that hard to fake bad swimming. She could just flail her arms wildly. And not kick at all, so she wouldn't have any speed. She'd splash a lot, to draw attention to herself, so all the girls would remember who had messed up, who had cost them the race. Thank goodness her hair streak was purple, brighter than some of the other girls' colors. It would help her stand out.

They were given black, regulation-style tanks to wear. Five looked at hers in distaste. "What's the opposite of sexy?" she asked. "Answer: this bathing suit."

Aly giggled, and Five winked at her. Amy watched the little interaction and frowned to herself. Some sort of friendship was obviously developing between the two clones. She didn't like it. Five was evil, and Five was also smart, which made her dangerous. If she got too chummy with Aly, she'd find out that Aly wasn't like the rest of them. And she wouldn't hesitate to tell the organization—who wouldn't have any reason to keep Aly around.

Then an awful realization struck Amy. Aly had no super-skills . . . no special talent for thinking, or seeing, or running—or *swimming*. *She'd* be the one who would stand out in the relay, the one who could lose it for them. And it would be Aly, Number Three, whom the others would want to vote off the team.

The clones were going back to the cabins to change into their suits and were supposed to meet at the dock. Amy had to come up with a plan, fast. "Alliance meeting," she hissed to Eight, and Eight ran to tell One. Amy looked around for Aly.

Aly was walking with Five. They were practically arm in arm, whispering, acting like best buds. Amy caught up with them.

"Three, can I talk to you for a second?" she asked.

"Sure," Aly said.

*"Privately?"*

Five gave her a reproachful look. "That's so childish, Seven. I'm not trying to steal your best friend. Why can't we all be friends?"

"Yeah," Aly said. "Five is fun! Hey, could she join our alliance?"

"What alliance?" Five asked, faking innocence.

There was no time for Amy to play games. "Like you don't know what I'm talking about," she said to Five. She grabbed Aly's hand and jerked her away. "Come on, this is important."

As soon as she knew Five wouldn't be able to hear, she lectured Aly. "Aly, you can't have everyone in an alliance, that's the whole point! Besides, she's got her own alliance!"

Aly looked confused. "I don't think I understand this whole alliance thing. Aren't we all supposed to be on the same team? Besides, you've got the wrong idea about her. Five is really nice. She hasn't said anything about me being slower than the rest of you. Maybe I'm getting stronger. I think that just being around you guys is making me more like you."

How dim could Aly be? Amy just hoped she'd understand the instructions she was about to get. "Listen, Aly, listen to me *very* carefully. I want to be voted off the team. But you're going to be the worst swimmer in the group."

Aly was actually offended. "How do *you* know? You've never seen me swim!"

Amy ignored that. "Aly, we have to change places. You'll be Seven, I'll be Three."

Aly stared at her for a moment. Then she smirked. "And you're supposed to be so smart! You've forgotten about something." She tugged at her blue hair. "This tells everyone who we are, remember?"

"I think I've got it covered," Amy said. She didn't add that she meant the statement literally.

Eight and One joined them in Amy's cabin. Amy searched her knapsack, and found what she needed. The bathing cap.

"I never wear bathing caps," Aly said.

"You will today," Amy told her. "But I'll be wearing it first."

She too hardly ever wore a bathing cap. Personally, she thought they looked goofy. But her mother had always insisted on them, particularly when they went to pools. "It's all the chemicals in the water," she used to tell Amy. "They wreck your hair." So Amy had gotten into the habit—whenever she packed a swimsuit, she packed a cap, too.

She pulled it on, stuffing her hair inside, checking to make sure her head was completely covered. As she did, she explained to all of them how the plan would work.

Aly wasn't too enthusiastic. "Okay, I'm not a good swimmer," she admitted. "But maybe I'm not the worst."

"You're the worst," Amy said flatly. "No offense, nothing personal, but you just don't have our genetic structure. Even if you *are* getting stronger." Which was ridiculous, of course—that was all in Aly's mind. Hanging out with people who had superior DNA didn't improve a person's genes. "And you don't want to get voted off, do you? You like it here! If you're the slowest, everyone will vote you off. Even your new friend, Five. Even me and Eight and One."

Luckily, Eight and One had caught on to the plan, and nodded vigorously in agreement. Aly muttered something about how this didn't sound like much of an alliance, but she finally agreed. One went to work on Aly's hair, braiding, brushing, and tucking it to hide the blue streak.

They all ran down to the dock where the relay was supposed to take place. Amy recognized the beach. This was where she'd arrived. In fact, she could see the boat, *Master of the Waves,* still docked nearby. But she couldn't think about that now. Since Four, Ten, and Twelve had been voted off, there were only five clones already in line when they arrived. Posing as Three, Amy stepped in between Two and

Five. About a quarter of a mile down the beach, she saw the Andys lined up. They had nine members left too.

Five whispered in her ear. "You're so smart to wear a cap," she said. "Salt water is terrible for your hair. I wish *I* had one."

Amy didn't respond. If Five thought she would be able to borrow Three's cap, she'd better forget it. The cap was going to someone else. Once Aly had dived and swum, her hair wouldn't stay in the style One had coaxed it into, and her blue would show.

Fortunately, no one had noticed the new hairstyle of Seven-really-Three—they were all so excited about the relay, no one was paying much attention to anyone but Cindy.

Cindy gave them instructions. "You run to the end of the pier, dive, swim to the raft out there, swim back, run back to the line and slap the hand of the next girl. No one can start off till her hand's been slapped. One, are you ready?"

"Ready," One called out. There was the sound of a whistle. Amy could see the first Andy take off at the same time as their own Amy One, but he hit the water first.

Amy One returned a few seconds behind the Andy.

She slapped hands with Two, and Two took off. Amy Two was really fast in the water, and she managed to creep ahead of the second Andy. As Three, Amy got into a running position even before Two returned to shore. She had to be as good or better than the others.

She dived into the water and began working her arms and legs furiously. Back at Parkside Middle School, there was a pool and all the students took swimming lessons in phys ed. She'd learned to swim *well*, not just fast. Of course, back at school she could never let herself swim with the speed she was really capable of. People might have noticed. In a way, she enjoyed this, knowing she could do her very best and no one would be shocked or amazed.

Coming back, she could see that Five looked surprised by her performance. Had she already figured out that Three wasn't up to the clone standard? Amy liked knowing she had just messed up any opinion Five had formed. She slapped Five's hand, maybe a little harder than she was supposed to.

She didn't remain with the girls who had already swum and were now out of line and cheering the others. She hurried to the back of the line.

She could feel the eyes of Nine—Annie Perrault—

on her. But she didn't let that stop her from speaking to Aly. "You said you wanted to borrow my bathing cap, didn't you? Because the salt's so bad for our hair?"

Aly looked sulky, and didn't say anything, but Eight piped up, "Yeah, she was just telling me that," and she hustled Aly out of the line and behind a large rock. Quickly Amy whipped off the cap and pulled it onto Aly's head.

"You know, I just might swim a lot better than you think," Aly grumbled.

But she didn't. She was just as bad and just as slow as Amy had hoped she would be. The two teams had been running almost neck and neck until "Amy Seven" dived in. By the time "Amy Seven" made it back to shore, her Andy rival was slapping the hand of another Andy.

Eight took her turn and dived in, but everyone knew the competition was over. Aly didn't need any hustling this time to come behind the rock and give the cap back to Amy. She certainly didn't want to take the responsibility for the big loss.

But Amy had no problem taking the blame, and none of the others seemed to have any problem laying it on her. After the sun went down, they met at the clearing and cast their vote. Amy wasn't at all surprised when Cindy announced that the majority had voted to send Number Seven off the island.

The two ski-masked men appeared and escorted her away from the clearing. She had no idea where she was going or what would happen to her.

But at least she'd be with Andy, here—or someplace else.

# seventeen

**T**he two men had strong grips on her arms, but Amy couldn't tell if they had super-strength or just the normal might of men their size. It didn't really matter either way. She didn't want to break free. She wanted to be with Andy, and they were going to take her to him. So she allowed herself to be pulled along and didn't put up any kind of struggle.

They were approaching the organization building. A Pink Smock was at the entrance, and she opened the door to them. The men led Amy down the hall to an elevator, which surprised her. As far as she could tell, this was a single-story building. There was only one button for the elevator, with an arrow pointing down.

So there were underground floors. She envisioned cold stone cells with iron bars. Possibly some torture equipment. And maybe an execution chamber, where the organization destroyed the rejected clones . . .

Trying to control her panic, Amy kept reminding herself of her strength, her speed, her ability to think and react quickly. If they planned to kill her, she had no intention of making it easy for them. Besides, there had to be some way to escape; she just had to stay alert. She had to be prepared for anything.

But nothing could have prepared her for what she saw when the elevator doors opened. She blinked rapidly and wondered if she might be hallucinating.

Because what she saw could have been a family room, a den, a rec room, in any suburban middle-class home. A comfortable-looking sofa and some easy chairs rested on a thickly carpeted floor. A giant-screen TV was showing an action movie. There was a Ping-Pong table on one side of the TV, a pool table on the other. A computer screen displayed an ocean scene with starfish and mermaids. Amy recognized the popular Pacifica game. Shelves on the walls held books, magazines, videos. A stereo system played hip-hop. A poster of Britney Spears hung on a wall. On another was a poster of James Van Der Beek, one of the cute actors from *Dawson's Creek,* and beside it, a poster of *NSYNC.

As for the occupants of the room, they looked perfectly content. Lounging in an easy chair, Aimee was thumbing through a *People* magazine. And Amys Twelve and Four were playing Ping-Pong. Two Andys were shooting pool; another was playing the computer game.

The Andy with the pink streak in his hair aimed his cue and hit two balls into a pocket.

"Good shot," the other Andy said.

A Ping-Pong ball sailed over Amy Twelve's head. "You're tilting your paddle back too far," she told Amy Four. "Hold it straight up."

"Okay," Four replied.

A gurgling noise from the computer announced that the player had just killed a shark.

Another Andy crossed the room and joined the two boys at the pool table. "Can I play?"

One of the boys handed him a stick. The new player pushed a lock of purple hair off his forehead.

"Andy!" Amy cried out.

All the boys in the room turned toward her. "Seven," her Andy said. "Hi."

She realized that the ski-masked men had let go of

her arms. She had an enormous urge to run to Andy, to throw her arms around him, to scream with joy that he was alive, that they were all alive. She didn't, of course.

"Are you okay?" she asked tentatively. "All of you, I mean?"

Aimee glanced up. "We're fine," she said, and returned to her magazine.

"I'm thirsty." That came from Andy Five, Andy with the purple streak, *her* Andy. "I'm going to get a Coke." He didn't ask if anyone else wanted one, not even Amy—who was suddenly aware of being thirsty.

"Can I have one too?" she asked.

"If you want," he said. "They're free." He left the room.

"Are you up for a game of Pacifica?" the boy at the computer asked her.

"No thanks," Amy said.

"Pool?" Andy with the crimson streak asked her.

"I don't know how to play pool," Amy said.

"It's easy," he said, but he didn't offer to teach her.

Unnerved, Amy glanced from clone to clone. What was going on here? Everyone looked so normal, so—so comfortable.

Amy Four was still having problems with her Ping-Pong shots. She hit a ball with force, and it struck Amy Twelve hard on the forehead. Amy winced for her.

She'd been hit with a Ping-Pong ball like that once, and she knew it could hurt.

Amy Twelve flinched and rubbed the spot on her forehead. "That hurt," she commented. "Don't swing so hard." But she wasn't upset, and Amy Four didn't even apologize. They continued to play.

Andy returned with a Coke—but only one. "Andy? You said you'd bring me a Coke."

"No, I didn't," Andy said. "I said you could *have* a Coke. They're in the kitchen." She'd never heard him be so impolite. But actually, he didn't sound rude— just matter-of-fact. He went over to the sofa and slumped down in front of the TV, his back to Amy and the others.

There was a bowl of candy on the railing of the pool table. Pink Andy stuck his hand in the bowl and crammed a fistful in his mouth. A second later, he started coughing violently. The other Andy was lining up a shot. No one paid any attention to the coughing Andy—whose face was now turning blue.

"He's choking!" Amy cried out. Still, nobody went to his aid. Amy ran over to him.

"Raise your hands," she yelled. She'd seen posters of the Heimlich maneuver and recalled the position. Grabbing him around the upper abdomen, she pulled up hard. The Andy coughed more loudly, and a nasty big chunk of chocolate popped out of his mouth. He took a couple of deep breaths.

"Are you okay?" Amy asked anxiously.

"Yeah," he said, his voice raspy. He picked up his cue. "Is it my turn?"

Amy's mouth dropped open. Wasn't he even going to thank her?

"Andy, Andy Five, give him some Coke," she ordered.

He actually looked away from the TV. "Why?" he asked.

"Because—because he was coughing, he almost choked to death; his throat must be all dry!"

Andy Five looked at her blankly. "No, I want my Coke," he said, and took another swig.

"Then get a Coke for him!"

"No," Andy said. "I want to watch the movie."

Amy looked around the room. "Could somebody please get him something to drink?"

No one budged.

"What's the matter with you all?" Amy cried out.

Aimee looked up again from her magazine with her usual bored expression. "What's the matter with *you*?"

Amy was speechless. Someone coming in spoke for her. "She's not as perfect as you are, Number Ten,"

Cindy said. "Not yet. Seven, will you come with me, please?"

Like she had a choice. On cue, the two ski-masked men took her arms again. She was led out of the "family room" and down the hall.

The room she was taken to didn't look at all cozy. The floors were tiled white and the concrete walls were undecorated. A metal table containing a sink and a cart with a small machine about the size of a microwave stood in the middle. White cabinets lined the walls, as did plastic folding chairs. The room had a sterile, medical look.

One of the men was rubbing his cheek. "I know they itch," Cindy said. "You can take off your masks now. I believe Amy has already seen your faces anyway. Haven't you, Amy?"

There didn't seem to be any point in denying it. But she didn't say anything as the ski masks came off and the two Mr. Devons stood before her.

"You're very clever, Amy," Cindy said. "Or maybe you're just more adventurous and curious than the others, I don't know. We haven't had the opportunity to run enough tests to ascertain the minor differences between you all."

Amy stared at her coldly. "I thought we were all supposed to be identically perfect."

"Perfection can vary," Cindy said. "And don't act so high-and-mighty, young lady, you're not as perfect as you could be. Those scientists at Project Crescent may have been the cream of the crop at that time, but we know more now."

"More about what?" Amy asked.

"Genetics," Cindy said. "And I say 'we' in a figurative sense. To tell you the truth, I don't understand it all myself. I'm not a scientist."

"But you *are* in the organization," Amy said.

"Yes, of course. Middle management, in a supervisory capacity."

Amy had no idea what that meant, but she didn't think it mattered. "How can you make us more perfect if you don't know anything about genetics?"

"It's not that difficult," Cindy said. "I didn't invent the procedure, but I can direct it. And I do know *something* about genetics. Probably more than you. For example, I know that the human genome consists of twenty-three pairs of chromosomes that contain the blueprint for human life."

Amy sneered. "Everybody knows that. We learn that stuff in eighth-grade biology."

Cindy was surprised. "Really? I don't remember learning that."

Amy didn't find her terribly bright. "You were probably too busy filing your nails," she couldn't resist adding.

Cindy frowned. "Don't be rude. I may have passed my peak as a supermodel, but I'm not *that* old."

That was when Amy noticed the small mole above Cindy's upper lip. Why hadn't she seen it before? Had Cindy been covering it with makeup? Slowly Amy drew in her breath.

"I know who you are," she whispered.

"No, you don't," Cindy said. "You just think you do. Honestly, Seven, do you think you and your little replicas were the first clones to be created in the universe? You're not that unique. Don't you read popular magazines or watch those TV shows like *Access Hollywood*? Haven't you ever wondered how those celebrities manage to be in so many places, go to so many parties, have their pictures taken so many times? Do you really think there are only five Spice Girls?"

"Four," Amy said faintly. "Ginger dropped out ages ago."

Cindy brushed that aside. "Well, there aren't only four. I don't know the precise number, but I'm sure there are at least ten. Of each."

"And you're a clone of—"

"Yes," Cindy said. "But our cloning was done long before the scientists knew how to reconfigure the DNA. We don't have your special skills."

"But you're not like the Pink Smocks," Amy said.

"No, they were a big foul-up," Cindy told her. "That was when the first attempts were made to play around with the chromosomes, and they didn't know what they were doing. We ended up with human robots."

Amy looked at the two silent Mr. Devons. "And these guys?"

"Like me," Cindy said. "Completely normal."

It was all Amy could do to keep from laughing at that remark. Cindy's next words put an end to her display of humor.

"No, we're not perfect like you, Amy. But as I said, you Amys and Andys aren't completely perfect either. Intellectually, you have the capacity to learn anything. Physically, you are at the peak of athletic capability and in superior health. But emotionally . . ." She shook her head sadly. "You're lacking."

"I have just as many emotions as anyone else," Amy said indignantly.

"That's precisely the problem," Cindy replied. "You can't be of any real use to us until we can stop those emotions from affecting your behavior. These petty loyalties and friendships, silliness, excitement, worries, depressions—they inhibit you, they affect your intellect and your energies. It's an impediment to fulfilling your mission in life."

It was starting to make sense to Amy. "So that's what emotional perfection is. No emotions at all."

Cindy seemed pleased by her comprehension. "Correct! You *are* clever. It took me much longer to make the others understand."

Amy's mouth was dry. She had a hard time getting out the next question. "How do you get rid of emotions?"

"It's actually not that difficult," Cindy said. "And don't worry, it's completely painless."

"That's nice to know," Amy said sarcastically.

Cindy laughed lightly. "Now, this is harder for me to explain because I really don't completely understand it. But you don't really need to understand it either. You see, it's something to do with the fact that humans carry the remnants of genes that were left behind ages ago, like hundreds of millions of years ago. And those remnants carry information about the earliest human behavior. I think this is all pretty new."

"I *know* that," Amy said. "I read newspapers."

"Anyway," Cindy continued, "those cavemen or ape-men or whatever they were didn't have a lot of complicated emotions. They could be afraid of something bigger and stronger that could hurt them. They could feel satisfaction when they killed something that threatened them or something they could eat. But that was about it! Nobody had the blues, nobody felt guilty. There were no nerds or creeps; no one was popular either. And most importantly, nobody cared about anyone else! Each individual only had to take care of himself. No one wasted their energies helping other people."

"Are you sure about that?" Amy asked. She didn't know that much about prehistoric civilization, but she'd always thought that caring and helping and teamwork was something basic.

"Yes, yes," Cindy said impatiently. "So, all we have to do is get that old gene remnant going again! That's what we've done with your brothers and sisters in the other room."

"So this is what happens to each clone who's voted off the island," Amy said.

"Well, not exactly. You see, we didn't know what we'd find in you. We thought some of you might need to have your genes dealing with strength and intellect worked on, but so far you haven't. And some of you may be more perfect emotionally than others. Like Number Nine."

Annie Perrault. Yes, after her experiences with Annie

in Paris, Amy could believe that she was born without feelings for other people.

"But don't you want us to fall in love and choose mates?" Amy asked. "Aren't we supposed to repopulate the earth with superior beings?"

"Oh, don't worry, you'll still mate," Cindy assured her. "You'll still feel, you know . . ." She giggled. "Sexy. Okay, let's get going here, I've got other things to do. Guys, you know the procedure. Seven, I'll see you later." And she strode out of the room.

One of the men went to the sink and washed his hands. The other opened a cabinet and took out some equipment.

"Are either of you the *real* Mr. Devon?" Amy asked urgently. "The one who knows me? Were you the assistant principal at Parkside Middle School? Someone, answer me! Can't you guys talk?"

"Sit down," one of the men said, indicating a plastic chair. The other one held out a paper cup of water in one hand and a small pink pill in the other.

"Take this, Seven," he said. "It will help you relax and you won't feel a thing."

Amy took a deep breath. Now was the time she had to figure out what kind of powers these guys had. She was going to have to try to take them on. She stepped toward the man with the cup and the pill. He glanced at her briefly, unalarmed.

"We may not have your superintelligence, Seven, but we're not stupid," he said, and nodded at the other man, who was now behind her. She turned and saw that he was holding a gun, and it was pointed right at her.

"Sit down," the man said again.

There was nothing in her physical being that would repel a bullet. But would they really kill someone who was so valuable to them?

The man with the gun read her mind. "We don't need all twelve of you, you know. Eleven would suit us fine."

Amy sat down. The man in front of her extended the cup of water and the pill toward her again. She accepted them. Now the man was placing electrodes on her head with some sticky gel stuff.

"The way this works, Seven," he said, "is that electric impulses shift the code in the prehistoric genome remnant. This dissolves the proteins that direct emotional response. Of course, the genes have to allow this to happen, and that's why you need to be completely relaxed, not frightened or even nervous. You have to be conscious, but without caring or feeling. Otherwise, emotions could disrupt the impulses, and the remnants won't be capable of devouring the proteins. And it could hurt."

"Hey, come on, we don't have all night," the other Devon said. "What are you telling her all that stuff for? She doesn't need to know. Besides, she can't be *that* smart."

"No big deal," he replied casually. "Just thought she might be curious. Take the pill."

The Devon with the gun had been partly right— Amy hadn't understood everything this Devon had just said. But she'd understood enough. She stared at him, and he stared right back at her, without blinking, with no expression at all. But she could have sworn she saw something in his eyes, something that told her there was a reason he'd given her that explanation.

Or maybe that was what she just *wanted* to believe. In any case, she had nothing to lose. So even though the man standing in front of her had his eyes fixed on her as she put the pill to her lips and opened her mouth, she let the pill fall down inside her T-shirt.

Had he seen her do that? How could he have missed it? But he said nothing. He went to the machine and adjusted some dials. After a moment, he looked back at Amy.

"How do you feel?"

Funny, how she almost automatically responded "Fine." But she kept her mouth shut.

"Amy? Are you feeling anything?"

"I feel nothing," she lied.

"Good," he said.

Then it dawned on her that he had called her Amy, not Seven. Amy. As if he knew her. Maybe he did.

It wasn't exactly painful, more like pressure. Like hearing a very loud, persistent noise that seemed to penetrate every cell in her body.

Emotions could disrupt the impulses, the man had said. She needed to think emotionally. Rapidly she tried to recall every major emotional moment of her life.

Winning the student council election at school. The first time Eric, her ex-boyfriend, had kissed her. Sad things too. She and her best friend, Tasha, not speaking. Leaving Eric behind at Wilderness Adventure. Despair, when she had had that awful fever and thought she'd lost her powers forever. Fear, when that girl who could make things move had tried to crush her under the gym bleachers. Mr. Devon had saved her that time.

Maybe he was saving her now.

The pressure was getting more intense. She concentrated, fighting back with the strongest emotions she could drum up. Love for her mother. The anger she felt at the organization. And grief, the terrible, heart-wrenching grief she had felt when dear Dr. Jaleski was murdered . . . she had to fight to keep the evidence of her emotion, tears, from springing into her eyes.

The whirring sound died down. One of the men was taking the sticky electrode things off her head.

"How do you feel?"

"Okay," she said.

"*What* do you feel?"

"I don't understand the question," she said.

It was the right answer. The two men escorted her out of the room and down the hall. Thoughts of Dr. Jaleski lingered in her mind, and she still felt like crying.

Thank goodness.

# eighteen

Amy had taken up permanent residence on the sofa in front of the TV. Videos had been playing all day. Right now she was watching a movie someone had put in the VCR. It was the first *Scream*, which Amy always considered the scariest of the three. She'd already seen all the movies they had to choose from, so she felt safe. She could easily control her reactions to the scenes that were emotional—sad, funny, scary, whatever. It might be harder not to show feelings if she were playing a game against another clone, or getting into conversations with them.

In particular, she had to stay away from Andy. Her

heart broke to see him like this, and it was all she could do to keep from crying each time she caught a glimpse of his face.

So she focused on the TV, on Drew Barrymore's face as she talked on the phone to a total stranger. The actress was smiling because she didn't know yet that the guy on the other end of the line was a killer. Aimee sat down beside Amy.

"Do you think she's a natural blond?"

"Who, Drew Barrymore?" Amy shrugged. "I don't know. Why?"

"I'm as pretty as she is," Aimee said. "I think I'd get her parts if I was blond. I guess I could dye my hair, but I wonder if there's a way to fix the genes that control your hair color."

"I suppose it's possible." Drew Barrymore was screaming now, and Amy remembered that the next scene had made *her* scream when she first saw it. She decided not to risk sitting through it again. A scream was a definite emotional response.

Luckily, there was a distraction. Cindy and one of the Devons came in wheeling a cart. "Bedtime snacks!" Cindy called out.

Last night's treats had been glazed doughnuts. Tonight's were frosted cupcakes with rainbow sprinkles. Obviously, the organization wasn't worried about their fat intake. Maybe they all had a special gene that kept them from gaining weight.

Nobody jumped up and down for joy at the sight of the cupcakes—they weren't capable anymore of strong feelings like that. But everyone could still appreciate taste, and all seven made their way over to the cart. There was milk, too. Amy had to admit that the organization was treating them quite well.

There were more than enough cupcakes to go around, but the clones were wolfing them down and going back for seconds. Amy thought they should save one for the new guy, the Andy who had been evicted by his team that evening. She couldn't suggest that, though. It would look like she cared about him.

He was having his "treatment." They were erasing his emotions, and, according to Cindy, supposedly doing a little coordination adjustment. Those minor differences between them had to be eradicated if they were going to be consistently perfect.

There was a single cupcake left, and one of the Andys reached for it.

"You can't have that," the crimson-streaked Andy said as he grabbed the other's wrist. "I want it."

"Well, it's mine," the other one said. "I'm still hungry."

"But if you eat it, there won't be another one for me."

Amy watched them, trying not to let her apprehension show. They weren't speaking emotionally, of course—just out of hunger, a desire for more cupcake. Would they resolve this dilemma intelligently, by cutting the cupcake in half and sharing it? Wasn't logic the opposite of emotion?

Apparently not. Brute force was the solution they chose. One Andy pushed the other away and grabbed the cupcake. The other one punched him in the face, causing him to drop the cupcake. They both dived for it, and ended up wrestling on the floor.

There were grunts and heavy breathing, but no show of passion, no anger, just a determination on the part of each boy to have the cupcake for himself. In alarm—but not showing it—Amy looked at Cindy and the Devon, but they simply watched with interest as the boys pounded on each other. Then Andy, *her* Andy, moved over to where they were fighting.

But Amy was disappointed. She was still hoping that Andy possessed some feeling, but he made no attempt to separate the fighting boys. Instead, he reached down, picked up the cupcake, and ate it.

Cindy beamed at him. "Excellent! That's just the kind of response we like to see. Just look out for yourself and take care of number one."

Amy's heart sank. Andy was empty, he felt nothing, he was just like the others.

Now that there was nothing to fight over, the boys stopped. And neither of them attacked Andy Five. The cupcake was gone, and an act of revenge or anger would have been an emotional response.

Then Amy heard something that drew her attention. There was a door by the TV. She'd never seen it opened and assumed it was a closet. Right now, it sounded like mice were scratching behind it. Amy just hoped it wasn't a rat. It would be extremely hard for her not to respond emotionally to that type of rodent.

The Devon went to the door and jerked it open. An Amy came tumbling out.

Not just any Amy clone. Amy recognized the blue streak in her hair. It was Aly.

And Aly recognized *her* streak. "Oh, Amy!" She rushed over and threw her arms around Amy. "You're alive, you're okay!"

Amy made herself go limp and resisted the urge to put her arms around Aly. Cindy strode over to them.

"What are you doing here, Three?" she demanded.

Aly bit her lip. "I ran away," she confessed. "I couldn't do the challenge today."

"The mountain climb," Cindy said.

Aly nodded. "I'm afraid of heights," she confessed.

"It was only because one of the boys fell that we won the challenge. But now the Amys are all mad at me. I know they're going to vote me off the next time we lose. And I found this tunnel. I thought it might take me off the island."

"Everyone gets voted off eventually," Amy Twelve pointed out. "Except the winner. You're not the strongest clone. If you hadn't been voted off tomorrow, it would have been the next day or the day after that."

"I didn't think about that," Aly admitted. She looked around the room. "Is this where you go when you're voted off? It doesn't look so bad. Ooh, I *love* Ping-Pong. Who wants to play?"

"Not now, Three," Cindy said briskly. "Since you're here, you might as well have your treatment now."

Aly looked nervous. "What kind of treatment?"

"It's nothing to worry about," Cindy assured her. "All the others here have undergone the treatment. It's to help you achieve a higher level of perfection. It's nothing bad, is it, girls?"

Ten, Twelve, and Four all shook their heads. Seven—Amy—couldn't move, could barely breathe. What was going to happen to Aly? She wasn't one of them, she didn't have their genetic makeup. There was no telling what the treatment would do to her. If she survived it . . .

As for Aly, her worried expression disappeared, and she didn't look nervous anymore. Amy had a feeling she knew what was going on in Aly's mind. Aly thought the treatment would make her like them, like a real Project Crescent clone. Perfect.

Now Cindy was hurrying her away. And there wasn't a thing Amy could do.

# nineteen

"What doesn't kill you makes you stronger."

Amy had heard that expression before but didn't remember where. In any case, it came back to her the next day as she watched Aly, Number Three-but-really-Thirteen, bounce around the basement room.

Whatever treatments had been given to Aly, they hadn't killed her. But she wasn't reacting like the other clones, either. She was too excited.

"Look at me, look at me," she kept crowing, and then she would demonstrate something she could do now that she hadn't been able to do before. Like lift something heavy. Like stand on her head, balancing herself with one hand. Like run across the room, take a flying leap, and jump over the long cart that held the remains of breakfast. She kept challenging people to arm-wrestle, giggling maniacally when she beat them.

If the others had cared, if they could feel anything, she would be getting on their nerves big-time. Mostly, they just ignored her. But Cindy watched Aly's antics with a curious expression.

"Something's off," Amy heard her say to one of the Devon clones. "She's not quite right. I don't like the way she's behaving."

"Wanna arm-wrestle?" Aly was asking one of the Andys now. He pushed her aside—not with anger, but just because she was standing in his way.

She was in *everyone's* way. With her genetic structure, the treatments had not only given her increased strength and flexibility, it had affected her energy, her attitude, her mood. She was on top of the world and she was all over the place.

"Look at me, look at me," she kept crying out, like a three-year-old on a playground. And then she'd do some dumb trick, something she hadn't been able to do the day before. Juggle plates. Perform back flips. Play an entire game of pool in two minutes, getting every ball into the right pocket with one little jab of the stick. Toss darts and hit the bull's-eye every time.

"Is it some sort of cell acceleration?" Cindy pondered aloud. "Will she burn herself out?"

The Devon had no answer.

With her face impassive, Amy examined that particular clone. Was he the Devon who had been in Aly's treatment session? Was he the same one who had been with Amy in hers? There was no way of knowing. Nothing distinguished the men. They didn't wear ski masks underground, and they both wore camouflage. Sometimes, when no one was watching, Amy would search their eyes for some kind of spark, some light, that might tell her this was the Devon she felt she had communicated with. But there were no clues there.

Now Aly had gotten into the utensils, and she was juggling knives. Cindy ordered the Devon to put a stop to that.

"You're not invincible," she told Aly sternly as the man took the knives away from her. "This is too dangerous. A sharp knife can still pierce your skin and injure you."

Aly wasn't put off by the comment. "I can do *anything*," she sang out, and started doing back flips again. In the process, she knocked over some dishes and they broke on the floor.

"She needs to work off energy," Cindy said abruptly. "Maybe they could all use some exercise." She clapped her hands. "Everyone, attention, please! We're going outside for a walk."

Amy worked at not letting the sudden lifting of her spirits show. Outside. A chance to escape? A chance to alert the Amys and Andys who were still out there? Maybe, maybe not. If she took any kind of action at all, it would show that she still had feelings, that she still cared about them. If she was caught, she'd be sent back for more treatment, and the next Devon might make sure she took the pill.

She couldn't plan anything; she didn't know where the walk would take them. She would just have to stay alert and be ready. If there was a possibility of escape, she'd have only the one chance.

They went up the stairs and out the front door. Cindy arranged them in two lines. Five Andys, five Amys. A Devon at the front of each line. A Pink Smock bringing up the rear. Cindy led them into the woods.

Amy kept glancing at the Andy who walked alongside her, Andy Five with the purple streak. She thought about the moments, the scary, dangerous, happy, sad moments that they'd spent together, and with each thought she felt a pang. She almost envied him for not being able to care anymore

Everyone walked at the same pace—except Aly. Aly skipped, Aly hopped, Aly was in perpetual motion and operating on a faster speed than the rest of them. She was another kind of person. And she was making Amy very nervous.

At one point, Aly jumped onto a rock and beat her chest like Tarzan. She issued an ear-splitting, inhuman screech, so loud that a huge flock of birds rose out of a tree in panic. The others continued to walk, and Aly caught up with them and took her place in line. But a moment later, she did something else crazy. Each time Aly got out of line, a Pink Smock or a Devon would shove her back. Aly just laughed—and that action, that show of emotion, made her even stranger.

"Aly, don't laugh," Amy said in a low voice, but Aly ignored her.

They were passing around some especially tall trees when she broke out of line again. This time, she leaped up and grabbed a tree limb. Dangling a few feet above the ground, swinging her legs, she yelled, "Look what I can do!"

The two lines stopped moving. "Get down from there," Cindy said.

"No," Aly replied. And before Cindy or anyone else could intervene, Aly started to climb the tree.

She was like a monkey, agile and fearless, leaping from limb to limb, climbing higher and higher. Amy watched with concealed concern as Aly grabbed limbs that looked too weak to support her. She wished Cindy would send her after Aly to drag her down. She couldn't do that on her own—it would show that she cared.

But when she heard an ominous crackle, she had to do something. Trying to look casual, she stepped out of the line and positioned herself at a particular point under the tree, so that when the branch broke and Aly came tumbling down—as Amy had guessed she would—Amy broke her fall and saved her from breaking a bone.

Amy herself was knocked down by Aly's weight. And it hurt. But at least Cindy couldn't tell that she'd acted intentionally.

"You were lucky Seven was standing there," she fumed at Aly. "You could have been hurt!" Aly just dusted herself off and laughed.

They were heading down to a beach now. Once they hit the sand, the pace slowed. Amy took advantage of the opportunity to step back and pulled Aly with her for a private word.

"Aly, listen to me," she said in a rush. "The treatment's made you stronger, as strong as the rest of us. And I know you feel like you're indestructible, but believe me, you're not. You can still be seriously hurt; you can still be killed!"

Aly stared at her. Then she grinned, in an ugly way.

"You know what, Amy? You're jealous! I'm as good as you are now. No, I'm better, and you don't like that. You can't boss me around anymore. I'm more perfect than you are!"

"Aly, that's not true," Amy protested, but Aly pushed her away.

"You said I couldn't swim like the rest of you. Well, watch this!" With that, Aly ran out toward the ocean.

"Stop!" Cindy yelled, and the two Devons ran after her. But Aly was fast now, as fast as any other Amy, and it wasn't long before she was a mere speck on the waves. The Devons remained on shore. Unwilling to get wet? Unable to swim? Who knew?

Amy could get her back. Any one of the Amys or Andys standing on the beach could rescue her and pull her to shore. But nobody moved, because nobody cared. And Amy wanted to cry, because she did care.

Aly couldn't get too far. She would drown out there. And Amy couldn't bear it. She would have to go after her, even if it meant betraying herself.

But then something about the speck changed. It was getting bigger. Aly was swimming back to shore. Amy remained still, her eyes glued to the swimmer.

Then Aly was back on shore, breathing hard but triumphant. "Did you see me? Did you see me? I swim better than anyone!"

Cindy was fed up with Aly's antics. "We're going back now," she told them. She assigned the Devon clones to take Aly's arms and keep her from fooling around.

When they approached the organization building, a third Devon was at the door. He opened it, and the two lines began to enter. That was when Aly broke free.

She leaped onto a window ledge.

"This is ridiculous," Cindy said to the Devons. "You must have done something wrong in her treatment. She's completely out of control. We're going to have to get rid of her."

"The organization won't like that," a Devon replied. "They want a dozen of each."

Aly had climbed to the top of the building by now. She was on the roof, and then she started to climb the water tower.

"Maybe she'll fall off and save us all a lot of trouble," Cindy commented.

Aly was on top of the water tower now. She stood poised on the edge of the tank, her arms outstretched.

"Watch me, watch me," she screamed. "I can fly!"

Amy caught her breath. She envisioned Aly sailing off the tank, over the edge of the roof. She would fall to earth headfirst.

No one's head was hard enough to survive that. Not

even a clone with accelerated cellular growth. Her skull would shatter on impact.

And she was really, truly crazy enough to believe that she could fly. It was written all over her face as she stood at the edge of the tank and flapped her arms up and down.

"Look at me! Look at me!"

With everyone's eyes on Aly, no one had noticed that an Andy had slipped out of line. Amy, Number Four, was the first to spot the boy with the purple streak in his hair, climbing onto the roof behind Aly. She pointed, and now everyone saw him.

"Andy," Amy whispered under her breath.

Andy tiptoed across the roof. Then he climbed the water tower at lightning speed and grabbed Aly around the waist. Aly shrieked and tried to beat him off, but Andy was stronger.

"What is he doing?" Cindy wondered out loud.

Amy knew. And she felt brave enough to say it. "He's saving her."

One of the Devons spoke. "That can't be true. You don't save someone if you don't care about other people."

"He cares," Amy said simply. "And so do I." With that, she ran over to the side of the building where Andy was bringing Aly down. She was ready to grab

Aly's hand as Andy lowered her to the window ledge. But Aly kicked in the window, smashing the glass, and pulled Andy in with her. Amy leaped up to follow them.

She ran after Aly and Andy, who were still hand in hand and rushing down a hallway. Aly didn't seem to be struggling. Andy was heading toward some stairs Amy hadn't noticed before, stairs that led to the underground level. Amy caught up to them as they reached the door Aly had come through into the cozy family room.

With his free hand, Andy jerked the door open. By now, Amy could hear the footsteps running after them. They had to move fast.

The door revealed a tunnel. It was dark and narrow. They ran single file, for what seemed like a mile. "You didn't take the pill," Amy gasped to Andy as they tore through the passage. "You had the good Devon, and he let you drop the pill, right?"

"There was no good Devon," Andy replied breathlessly. "I just faked him out."

This was not the time or place to argue about that. "How did you fight off the impulses?" she wanted to know. "How did you hold on to your emotions?"

"I thought about you," Andy said.

At that moment, with his words, the emotions that filled her gave her complete reassurance that her ability to feel hadn't been damaged at all.

The tunnel began to slope upward, and they had to get down on their hands and knees to climb through. In front of her, Aly was starting to slow down. Her breath was coming out in short, harsh gasps. Andy heard it too. He reached behind and grabbed her hand. He pulled, Amy pushed. The incline became steeper. And then Amy heard a thump.

"It's closed off!" Andy cried out. "It feels like metal!"

"Knock," Aly said.

"What did you say?" Andy asked.

"It's a *door*, stupid. Knock!"

Andy knocked. Peering above, Amy could see a ray of light as the closure lifted. Then there were hands, reaching down, pulling them up and out. Amy was the last to find herself standing on a real floor, inside a cabin.

Face to face with Amy, Number Five.

# twenty 20

"Good job," Five said to Aly.

"Thank you," Aly replied.

Amy felt her stomach drop. She looked at Andy. He was totally confused.

"What's going on here?" Andy wanted to know.

"It was a setup," Amy told him grimly. She nodded toward Five. "This one collaborates with the organization. She got chummy with my *ex*-friend Aly here and convinced her to come over to their side. And we played right into their hands."

Stricken, Aly gasped. "No, Amy, that's not true! She's going to help us all!"

Amy groaned. "Aly, you are *so* gullible."

Five turned to Amy. "And you're so—okay, not stupid, but not as smart as you think you are."

"I *saw* you in the hospital," Amy snapped. "I *heard* you. You were plotting with that doctor. You were on their team!"

Five glared right back at her. "Haven't you ever heard of double agents? I let them think I was on their side so I could find out what they were up to! How do you think we all managed to get out of there? And here, they trusted me, so they gave me the cabin with the tunnel to the organization headquarters. I sent Aly to show you the way back."

From under the floor, they all heard sounds. Five spoke to Andy. "Help me with this." She began pushing a large chest onto the spot they had come through. Still confused, Andy looked at Amy.

"I don't get it," he said. "Should I do what she says?"

"We don't have much time," Five told him. "If they can get all the converted Amys and Andys to push, they can open the door even with the trunk on it. Hurry up!"

Something about her assertive tone made Andy follow her orders—and kept Amy from trying to stop him. They pushed the trunk into position.

"Let's go," Five said.

"Go where?" Amy wanted to know.

"To the boat."

Amy hesitated. But Five was losing patience.

"Look, Seven, you may think you're hot stuff, but you can't be on top of everything all the time. Now, you either trust me about this, or you find your own way off this island."

Five ran out of the cabin, with Aly, Andy, and Amy close behind. Aly was having a hard time keeping up, though.

"I'm slowing down," she moaned.

"The medication's wearing off," Five said. "I told you that would happen."

"Can you give me more?" Aly pleaded.

"No, it would be too much for your system," Five said. "You'd burn out."

"Get on my back," Andy ordered Aly.

With Aly riding piggyback, they were able to make it to the beach in less than a minute. There, on a stretch of powdery sand, six Amys and seven Andys were waiting. Most of them started cheering when they saw the group coming toward them. Eight, the New Yorker, let out a whoop, ran to them, and threw her arms around Amy.

One Amy was not happy.

"But you are all so wrong!" Number Nine declared in her charming French accent. "Do you not understand? We are the elite, we are the hope of the future! We can change the world! We can *rule* the world!"

She followed them as they all ran down the beach to the pier, where *Master of the Waves* was still docked. Splashing out into the water, one by one they made their way to the rope ladder that hung down the side of the boat.

Then a warning went up from one of the Andys. "They're coming!"

Amy turned and saw figures coming onto the beach. Cindy, the Devons—she counted three—plus four Pink Smocks, four Andys, and three Amys. Annie Perrault was running toward them, yelling and pointing to the boat.

"Hurry, get on the boat!" Five screamed.

Meanwhile, Cindy was giving orders to her group. "Stop them," she shouted.

The Devons and the Pink Smocks followed orders. They splashed into the water and started toward the group trying to get aboard the boat. But there was nothing superhuman in those clones, and they made their way slowly.

It was their own clones they had to worry about. "Go after them," Cindy was yelling.

But there seemed to be a problem. The converted

Amy and Andy clones didn't run into the ocean. Amy heard Number Nine screaming, "Come on, let's go after them," but none of the other clones were moving.

They'd reached the rope ladder. Aly started up; Andy waited for Amy to go before him. Five was watching the slow approach of the Devons and Pink Smocks. She didn't seem terribly concerned.

"I don't understand," Amy said. "Why aren't the other clones coming after us?"

"Because they don't care," Five said.

"Huh?"

"They only care about themselves. They don't want to get wet and muddy and they certainly don't want to fight for the organization." She smiled. "You see, the organization didn't take that into consideration. Loyalty—it's an emotion."

Five was right, and very smart to have figured that out. Amy looked at her with new respect. She started up the ladder; Andy followed and Five came last. They were all on deck now. But there was still a problem.

"The boat runs by remote control," Amy told Five. "How can we make it move?"

This time Five didn't have a quick answer. The look of total confidence on her face began to evaporate.

Amy surveyed the water between the boat and the shore. The Pink Smocks and Devons were getting closer.

Number Nine was coming too, and Cindy was still try-ing to convince the other clones to go after the boat. She and the others were sitting ducks.

And then she saw someone else—another Devon, a fourth one. He was standing on the shore, looking at them. Even from this distance, Amy thought she could make out a light in his eyes, the hint of a smile on his lips.

He raised his hand—revealing a small black object in his palm. He pointed it toward the boat and pressed a button. The boat began to move.

Five was stunned. "Why did he do that?"

It was Amy's turn to smile. "Trust me, Five. I'm on top of this." And it was the other girl's turn to look at *her* with respect.

Andy put his arm around Amy's shoulders, and the others gathered around. There was no million-dollar reward waiting for them. But they were all survivors.

## Memo from the Director

Unanticipated consequences have prevented the island mission from becoming a complete and unqualified success. However, it is not to be considered a failure. The organization has retained four males and four females. This may be sufficient to achieve our goal.

# Don't miss

# *replica*

## #19
## Dreamcrusher

A sudden storm at an end-of-summer back-to-school beach party sends Amy scrambling for cover—but a bolt of lightning hits her as she runs. Next thing she knows, she wakes up in a hospital emergency room. Everything's fine. Or is it?

Suddenly Amy can hear more than she'd like to.

She can see things that disturb her.

In fact, all her senses are on edge.

At first Amy thinks it's way cool to have extrasensory abilities—until they become more like a curse than a gift. Now she just wants to shut them down for good!